TIES THAT BIND

RUTHLESS SINNER'S MC

L. WILDER

Ties That Bind
Ruthless Sinners MC Series- Book 1
Copyright 2020
L. Wilder- All rights reserved.

Without limiting the rights under copyright reserved above, no part of this publication or any part of this series may be reproduced without the prior written permission of both the copyright owner and the above publisher of this book.

This book is a work of fiction. Some of the places named in the book are actual places found in Nashville, Tennessee. The names, characters, brands, and incidents are either the product of the author's imagination or are used fictitiously. The author acknowledges the trademarked status and owners of various products and locations referenced in this work of fiction, which have been used without permission. The publication or use of these trademarks is not authorized, associated with, or sponsored by the trademark owners.

This e-book is licensed for your personal enjoyment only. This e-book may not be re-sold or given away to other people.

L. Wilder be sure to stay connected-

Social media Links:

Facebook: https://www.facebook.com/AuthorLeslieWilder

Twitter: https://twitter.com/wilder_leslie

Instagram: http://instagram.com/LWilderbooks

Amazon: http://www.amazon.com/L-Wilder/e/B00NDKCCMI/

Bookbub: https://www.bookbub.com/authors/l-wilder

Sign up for L. Wilder's Newsletter: http://bit.ly/1RGsREL

Cover Design: Mayhem Cover Creations

Image: Wander Book Images

Model- Griffin

Editor: Lisa Cullinan

Proofreader- Rose Holub @ReadbyRose

Proofreader: Honey Palomino

Teasers & Banners: Gel Ytayz at Tempting Illustrations

Personal Assistant: Natalie Weston PA

>Catch up with the entire Satan's Fury MC Series today!
>All books are FREE with Kindle Unlimited!

Summer Storm (Satan's Fury MC Novella)

Maverick (Satan's Fury MC #1)

Stitch (Satan's Fury MC #2)

Cotton (Satan's Fury MC #3)

Clutch (Satan's Fury MC #4)

Smokey (Satan's Fury MC #5)

Big (Satan's Fury #6)

Two Bit (Satan's Fury #7)

Diesel (Satan's Fury #8)

Blaze (Satan's Fury MC- Memphis Book 1)

Shadow (Satan's Fury MC- Memphis Book 2)

Riggs (Satan's Fury MC- Memphis Book 3)

Murphy (Satan's Fury MC- Memphis Book 4)

Gunner (Satan's Fury MC- Memphis Book 5)

Gus (Satan's Fury MC- Memphis Book 6)

Rider (Satan's Fury MC- Memphis Book 7)

Day Three (What Bad Boys Do Book 1)

Damaged Goods- (The Redemption Series Book 1- Nitro)

Max's Redemption (The Redemption Series Book 2- Max)

Inferno (Devil Chasers #1)

Smolder (Devil Chaser #2)

Ignite (Devil Chasers #3)

Consumed (Devil Chasers #4)

Combust (Devil Chasers #5)

My Temptation (The Happy Endings Collection #1)

Bring the Heat (The Happy Endings Collection #2)

His Promise (The Happy Endings Collection #3)

❦ Created with Vellum

PROLOGUE

I never considered myself to be a player. Sure, I appreciated the company of a beautiful woman from time to time, but I never led any of them on. I didn't make empty promises or insinuations that I was looking for anything more than a good, hard fuck. Never had to. I'd always made sure the women I hooked up with knew exactly what they were getting into—a night of the best sex they'd ever had—followed by my immediate exit.

JUST TO BE CLEAR, I wasn't some lost soul who was searching for the love I never got as a kid. Nothing happened to me in my past that fucked me up and I wasn't able to shake it. I wasn't seeking some kind of validation or affection to heal my wounded heart. I was simply a man who didn't want any complications. I didn't have time for it and most likely never would.

. . .

Don't get me wrong. There were times when I found myself wondering if I was missing out on something—like the night my brothers and I had gone to Memphis to party with the brothers of Satan's Fury. While I was there, I'd met a woman who made me question my wicked ways. She was beautiful, but it was her spirit and strength that got to me the most. For the first time in my life, I'd actually considered a life full of complications, but then I discovered she belonged to someone else. Normally, that wouldn't have been enough to stop me from trying to make a play for her, but she was tied to Clay, my president's nephew, which made her completely off-limits. I'll admit, after meeting Landry Dawson, I started to wonder if I'd ever find a woman to claim as my own.

HAWK

*L*oyalty. Faith. Family. Those are the ties that bind. I'd never realized just how important those ties were until I joined the Ruthless Sinners MC. With them, I'd found a family who'd stand by my side when things went south, as I would them. No matter the circumstance, our loyalty to one another never wavered. We were family—our ties stronger than blood—and I'd never been prouder than the day my brothers voted me in as their sergeant-at-arms. I'd always done my best to fulfill my duties, even when it wasn't easy—just like tonight.

The brothers had gathered at Stilettos, the club's main front business, to check out the new strippers our manager had just hired. The guys were eager to see the fresh meat before we opened for the night. They looked like kids on Christmas morning when the music started playing and Candy stepped up on the stage. The hot blonde was all smiles as she made her way over to the pole, and of course, all the guys started hooting and hollering the second she slipped off her halter top. I, on the other hand, just wasn't into it. Don't get me wrong, it wasn't that I didn't find Candy attractive, I did. Hell, when it came to chicks, it didn't matter if they were tall, short, thick, or thin, I could find something appealing about all of them.

But tonight, I had more important things on my mind than getting laid. I was pissed that I hadn't heard back from Danny—the club's supplier. He and I needed to have words, and he knew it.

I reached into my back pocket for my phone and was about to dial his number when I heard Axel ask, "Something up?"

"Just waiting to hear back from Danny."

No one would ever guess that Axel had a good ten to fifteen years on me. The guy was built like an ox and could take any asshole who was stupid enough to go up against him—which was one of the many reasons he was the club's VP. Axel was aware of the issue with Danny, so I wasn't surprised when he asked, "You think we should have Shotgun pay him a visit?"

"Definitely." While Stilettos brought in a good bit of cash for the club, it was nothing compared to the money the girls brought in when they sold coke to our customers. The club had been using Danny for years. We'd done our homework, knew he was supplying for several others in the area, and they'd been pleased with not only his reliability but his product. Everyone knew he wasn't the main supplier, that he was getting the take from a distributor in Texas, but he'd always been dependable when it came to keeping up with our supply and demand. But recently, it seemed we were having to deal with one fuck-up after the next. It started with a couple of late deliveries, which quickly progressed into him missing one altogether. That in itself should've been enough for us to walk away, but we were in a bind for time and bought one last shipment from him—one big fucking shipment that cost over two hundred grand to get our hands on.

We'd assumed it would be our last time having to deal with Danny ... until we discovered that part of the shipment was counterfeit. That discovery hadn't come until days later, when we started breaking down the shipment. Viper was pissed to find that over half of the take was counterfeit, especially since it was the half we hadn't tested on delivery. That was on us, but the fact remained, Danny was the one who'd swindled us. He'd crossed a line, a big fucking line, and he damn well knew it. The motherfucker knew he would have to answer to the club for what he'd done. That's why he was laying low and hadn't returned any of my fucking calls. I glanced over at Shotgun, the club's enforcer, and Rafe, then shook my head when I saw him gawking at Candy's ass as she stepped off the stage. "The sooner the better."

"Can't disagree with you there." A concerned look crossed his face. "This whole thing is fucked up."

"Yeah, but one way or another, we'll take care of it."

"I don't doubt that ... It's just ... we need to keep in mind there's the possibility that Danny didn't know the product was counterfeit."

"Maybe, but there's also the possibility that the asshole just got fucking greedy and was hoping to pull one over on us." I reached for an Ultra-Light and took a long pull. "But I hope, for his sake, that's not it."

"Yeah. If that's the case, it won't end well for him."

"Well, we won't know for sure until Shotgun gets his hands on him."

Axel glanced over at Shotgun, snickering as he watched our brother pull Candy onto his lap. "As amped up as those two are right now, they're liable to kill the stupid sonofabitch before he ever gets a chance to talk."

I chuckled as I stood and walked over to Shotgun. Our enforcer wasn't a small man, but he wasn't as big as one might think. He was tall with an athletic, muscular build, and he could handle himself just as well as the rest of us, but his physical appearance had nothing to do with why he'd been chosen as the club's enforcer. The choice was simple really. Shotgun had talents the rest of us just didn't have. He was missing that part of the brain that made a man feel empathy or the slightest bit of remorse for the pain he dished out, especially when that person had gone against the club. When vengeance took over, torture and all the other things that might make another man squeamish wouldn't affect him in the least. There was nothing he wouldn't do when it came to extracting the intel we needed from a particular individual. That, and the fact that the man could do some real damage with a shotgun, like *wipe-out-an-entire-army* kind of damage, made him a force to be reckoned with. With his particular skill set, the guy was invaluable to the club, and I knew I could trust him to figure out what the hell was going on with Danny. Candy was trying to squirm out of his lap when I said, "'Gun ... I got something I need you to do."

"All right." He let out a deep sigh as he lifted Candy off his lap. "What do you need me to do?"

"I want you and Rafe to head over to Danny's place and see if you find any sign of him."

"And if I do?"

"Bring his ass to the club. We have things to discuss with him."

His brows furrowed. "This about his last shipment?"

"Yeah." I crossed my arms as I continued, "It's time he gave us some answers about what the fuck is going on."

"Understood."

"He's gotta know we're gonna be looking for him, so watch your back," I warned. "You can never be too careful in situations like these."

"I got it covered."

I watched as he motioned over to Rafe, letting him know it was time to go. Rafe took one last glance at the new chick on the stage before standing and following Shotgun out the door. Once he was gone, I turned my attention to the stage, watching as our second new stripper, Kaleigh Jo, removed her top and tossed it to the guys. Like Candy, she was a pretty girl, young with a killer body, and the lights shimmered against her mocha-colored skin. There was no doubt that the girl had mad skills when it came to working the pole. Hell, she had all the guys completely captivated, including me. It was one of the reasons I hadn't noticed that Lisa, Stilettos' bartender, had come up next to me until she asked, "Enjoying yourself there, handsome?"

"Hmph." I grunted. "I'm doing all right. You?"

"Same." She inched closer as she purred, "I'd be a lot better if you paid me a visit later tonight. I could use the company."

Lisa was a beautiful woman, tall with an hourglass figure and dirty-blonde hair, and I wouldn't lie, I'd considered hooking up with her in the past but never followed through. She busted her ass at work, did whatever she had to do to take care of her kid, and something in my gut told me she was interested in more than one night. Much more. That wasn't going to happen. Not with me. So, I simply smiled and said, "I'm not the kind of company you need or want, doll."

"I don't know about that." She placed the palm of her hand on my chest and provocatively whispered, "I think you're exactly the kind of company I'm looking for."

I took hold of her wrist and gently removed her hand. "As tempting as it might be, it's not going to happen."

"Why not?" A mix of hurt and anger crossed her face. "You're not attracted to me?"

"Didn't say that, Lisa. You're a beautiful woman. You know that." I let go of her wrist and took a step back. "Set your sights on a man who can give you what you really need, 'cause trust me when I say, it isn't me."

Before she could respond, I turned and headed over to Axel. After I let him know that I was going back to the clubhouse to check in with Viper, I went out to the parking lot and got on my Harley. Moments later, I was in the thick of Nashville traffic. Rush hour had come and gone, but there were still plenty of cars on the road. It was Nashville after all—the homeplace of the Ryman and the Grand Ole Opry, where many country music legends got their start. People from all over the world visited Music City, making Nashville one of the fastest-growing cities in Tennessee, which was always a good thing for a business like Stilettos. Over the past ten years, the strip club had doubled in size, and we were in the process of opening a second one closer to downtown. With all the red tape of zoning and permits, it was a lot to take on—which made the hassle with Danny all the more frustrating. We didn't have time for distractions, and I hoped that Shotgun and Rafe would be able to help us get some kind of resolution on this fucking thing.

When I got to the clubhouse, I found Viper sitting at the bar with Lynch and Menace. They were each drinking a cold one as they talked amongst themselves, but quickly grew quiet when I approached. Noting my expression, Viper asked, "You heard anything from Shotgun or Rafe?"

"Not yet." I took a seat next to him. "Shouldn't be much longer, though. Danny's place isn't far from here."

Lynch shook his head as he muttered, "Surely, the asshole isn't stupid enough to be at his place."

"I pinged his phone's location a few hours ago, and he was still there," Menace, the club's computer whiz, replied. "Well ... *his phone* was still there. I can't say the same for him."

"We'll know soon enough." Viper ran his hand over his beard with an unsettling grunt. "I gotta tell ya, I've got a bad feeling about all this. I'm thinking this thing goes a lot further than just Danny."

"Who else could be involved?"

"Danny's not big enough or smart enough to be leading the chain on this supply," Viper replied. "Besides, he doesn't have the balls to try and pull one over on us. He knows what we'd do to him."

"You're right about that," Lynch scoffed. "You thinking it's his supplier?"

"Don't know yet, but we're sure as hell gonna find the fuck out, and when we do, there's gonna be hell to pay," Viper growled. "Nobody pulls this kind of shit on the Sinners and gets away with it."

The room fell silent as we considered what Viper had just told us. The possibility of going to war with a drug lord wasn't an easy pill to swallow, especially considering the timing. Stilettos was booming, and we were under the gun to get the second club up and running. There wasn't time to deal with any distractions, which was one of the main reasons we'd decided to be done with Danny in the first place. We knew something was up with him but made the mistake of trusting him with one last delivery anyway. *That* mistake wasn't sitting well with Viper. He was a man who was always a step ahead. He caught problems before they happened, so it only made sense that all the unknowns of the situation were getting to him. We were all lost in our own thoughts when the back door of the bar flew open and Danny stumbled inside.

"What the fuck?" Viper roared as he shot up and rushed in that direction with the rest of us following closely behind. Danny's hands were bound behind his back, and he could barely see through his swollen eyes and the blood running down his face. Just as he was about to topple over and fall flat on his face, Viper grabbed him by the arm and shoved him into a chair. "Sit your fucking ass down and don't move."

Danny didn't speak. He simply lowered his head, cowering like a wounded animal. That's when I noticed his blood-soaked shirt. It didn't look like the blood had come from him, which left me wondering who the blood belonged to. I was just about to ask him when Shotgun appeared in the doorway, and like Danny, he was covered in blood. "Need help getting Rafe out of the truck."

"What the hell's going on?" Viper roared.

"That dumb motherfucker shot him!" Shotgun snarled.

Without another word, he turned and raced back towards his truck. Viper turned to Lynch and ordered, "You stay here with him. Menace, you go get Doc."

Menace nodded, then ran out of the bar while Viper and I went out to help Shotgun with Rafe. We found Rafe in the front seat, and a surge of adrenaline rushed through me as I noticed he had a bullet wound to the chest and another in his lower abdomen. His head was leaned back, and his white t-shirt was now completely drenched in blood. Unbuckling Rafe's seatbelt, Shotgun whispered, "All right, brother. It's time to get you inside."

Rafe was pale and clearly weak as he raised up and looked at Shotgun. "You can stop with all that worrying shit, brother. I'm gonna be fine."

"I know you are," Shotgun argued.

"And another thing"—Rafe winced as Viper helped Shotgun carefully lift him out of the truck—"it ain't your fault that dickhead shot me. No way you could've—"

"Enough of that," Shotgun interrupted. "You need to save your strength."

"I told you to stop that shit. I'm not dying. Damn." Rafe grunted as they started towards the door. "It's just a flesh wound."

I rushed over and opened the door for them. Once they were inside, I started to follow them but stopped when Shotgun looked over to me and said, "Gonna need you to go get the girl."

"The girl? What girl?"

"Says she's Danny's sister. She's still in the back, and be careful," Shotgun warned. "That one's a live wire."

With all the commotion, I hadn't seen anyone else in the back seat, but I took his word for it and went over to the truck. I opened the back door to find an extremely pissed off red-headed beauty sitting there with her arms bound behind her back and duct tape covering her mouth. She was wearing a pair of blue scrubs, and her hair was pulled back, revealing the clearest blue eyes I'd ever seen. They were beautiful, not just because of the color, but because of the fire hidden behind them—the kind of fire that could burn straight to one's very soul. Damn.

DELILAH

We all have those memories that are stronger and more vivid than others. They often rise to the surface when we least expect it—maybe in a dream or if we're having a bad day. For me, that memory had always been the day my mother finally got the courage to leave my father. I was only eight at the time, but even then, I knew the significance that day held. My father had never been one of those loving, doting husbands, nor was he a caring, understanding father. He was rarely even home, too busy gambling our money away instead of giving much thought to his family—and when he was, he'd be nothing but controlling and abusive, especially where my mother was concerned. She'd tried to make the best of it, doing everything she possibly could to make him happy and shielding us from the wrath of his uncontrollable temper. Unfortunately, as the years passed, it'd gotten harder and harder to please him, and even though she'd done everything she could to prevent it, his anger eventually became directed at my brother, Danny. It seemed like it was fine for my dad to beat the hell out of her, but the second she discovered that he'd put his hands on my brother, she was done. She had us pack our bags, and we headed to my grandmother's house.

My grandmother had been in a nursing home for a month, so Mom decided that we could stay there until she was able to get back on her feet. The house wasn't anything fancy, just an older three-bedroom home with room after room of antique furniture and tiny holes in the walls from where she'd hung our pictures all over the house, but I'd never felt so much at home as I did there. I could almost feel my grandmother's presence watching over us as we settled in and slowly turned the place into our own. Without even knowing it, she'd given us a chance at a fresh start—one without fear or regret. There was no more tiptoeing around my father, watching our every word or being quiet as church mice. We were finally free to breathe, and it was wonderful. I couldn't remember ever being happier than I was in that little house.

As I'd gotten older, I made a vow to myself to make the best out of the second chance my mother had given us. I graduated from college, earning a degree in health care, and had gotten a job at a nursing home, busting my ass in hopes of making my mother proud. I'd always hoped that my brother would do the same. Sadly, he hadn't. He didn't seem to care about anything, much less making anyone proud. I hadn't realized how bad things had gotten with him until the day he almost got us both killed.

I WAS JUST ABOUT to get off work when my mother called my cellphone. Normally, I wouldn't answer a call during work hours, but I'd already made my rounds and was gathering my things to go home. "Hey, Mom. What's up?"

"Have you heard from Danny?"

"No. Why?"

Her voice was laced with concern as she replied, "I've been trying to get ahold of him for weeks, but he hasn't returned any of my calls."

"You know Danny. He's probably just running around with his buddies or something," I tried to reassure her. "Who knows? Maybe he actually got a real job."

"I don't know, Delilah. It's not like him to go this long without answering my calls or texts. I'm really worried about him."

I knew what was coming. She was going to ask me to go see about him. I'd been working all day, my head was pounding and my feet were aching, and the last thing I wanted to do was go check in on my big brother. Before she could ask, I suggested, "You know, you could just go over to his place and see if he's there."

"I know and I would, but he gets upset when he thinks I'm meddling in his life." Knowing I'd failed, I cringed and waited for her to turn the tables on me. "I know you're busy with work, and I really hate to ask ... but could you go over there and check on him?"

"Yeah, I'll stop by his place on my way home from work."

"And you won't tell him that I sent you?"

"No, Mom, I won't tell him."

"Thank you, sweetheart. I knew I could count on you," she replied, sounding relieved.

"I'll call you when I know something more."

"I'll be waiting."

I hung up my phone and slipped it into my bag. After I grabbed the rest of my things, I headed up front to find Janet, the lead nurse, to let her know I was leaving for the day. As luck would have it, I found her sitting at her desk, working on the next week's schedule. She was deep in thought and hadn't realized that I was standing in front of her until I said, "Hey ... I'm calling it a day."

"Oh ... before you go, Carla has an appointment Tuesday afternoon." Janet was in her late forties, heavy-set with jet-black hair that she colored way too often. Her makeup was a bit overdone, but she was still a pretty lady with a warm personality to match. She'd always been very kind to me, always treating me and the other nurses with nothing but respect, so it was impossible not to like her. She gave me a slight smile and said, "I was hoping you'd be able to work late on Tuesday?"

"Sure, I can do it."

"Great!" She smiled. "I'll put you down."

"Sounds good." I turned to leave, and just as I was about to step through the door, I turned back and said, "Have a great night. I'll see you in the morning."

"You too."

I got in my car and started towards Danny's apartment. It wasn't anything special, just a one-bedroom with barely enough room for a bed and a sofa, but I had no idea how he paid for it. He hadn't had a real job in months, so I could only assume that my mother had been helping him out—which aggravated me to no end. Danny was more than capable of taking care of himself, and he certainly didn't need our mother giving him handouts. The thought was weighing on me as I pulled up to his apartment complex. I got out of my car and took a quick glance around but didn't see his truck in the parking lot. I was beginning to think I'd wasted a trip until I spotted his Dodge pickup parked a couple of blocks down the street. While that seemed a bit odd, I didn't stop to think about it. I wanted to check on him as quickly as possible, so I could get home and unwind for the day. I made my way up to his door, then knocked and waited for him to answer.

I hadn't been standing there long when I grew impatient and knocked a second time, only harder. I was almost positive that I'd heard him moving around in there, so I shouted, "Danny! I know you're in there! Open the stupid door!"

"Delilah?"

"Yeah! Who else would it be?" When the door flew open, I only got a quick glimpse of Danny's pale, panic-stricken face before he turned and rushed down the hall. "What's wrong?"

"I've run into a little trouble." I followed his voice into his bedroom and was surprised to see that there were various bags spread out across his bed. "I'm gonna have to get out of town for a little while."

"What are you talking about? What kind of trouble?"

"I don't have time to talk about it, Dee." He shoved the rest of his clothes into one of the duffle-bags and zipped it up. "I've gotta get out of here while I still can."

"You can't just walk out of here without telling me something, Danny," I fussed. "What have you gotten yourself into?"

He turned and grabbed a handgun out of his closet,

carefully slipping into the back of his waistband. "Nothing that I can't handle."

"What the hell, Danny!" I screeched. "You need a gun to 'handle' the situation?"

Before he had a chance to respond, there was a knock at the door. The blood drained from Danny's face as he muttered, "Fuck. They're here."

"Who?"

"You need to get out of here, Delilah ... *Now!*"

Panic surged through me as I heard him cock his gun. "Where the hell am I supposed to go? We're on the third damn floor!"

Whoever was standing at the front door started pounding on it as they shouted, "We know you're in there, Danny. Open the goddamn door before we knock the motherfucker down."

"Oh, my god, Danny! Who is that?"

Without answering, he grabbed me by the arm and shoved me into the corner. "Stay here. Don't move until I come to get you. Understand?"

I nodded, then watched as my brother stepped out of the room, closing the door behind him. Moments later, I heard the front door open and then booming voices filled the small apartment. Hoping to figure out what the hell was going on, I leaned towards the door and tried to listen to what they were saying, but with all the screaming and shouting, I couldn't understand a word. I was a nervous wreck and nearly hit full-blown panic mode when I heard one of the men shout, "Put that fucking thing away, Danny."

Remembering that he'd gotten a gun out of his closet, I quickly opened the door and found my brother with his gun aimed at two menacing looking men wearing biker vests. I knew Danny rode a motorcycle with a group of friends, but I'd never seen these guys before. They were much rougher, meaner looking, than any of the guys Danny rode with, and if their fierce expressions were any indication, they were pissed that Danny had drawn his weapon. I was just about to call out for him to stop when he snarled, "Already told you ... I didn't have nothing to do with that shit."

"Well then, you shouldn't have a problem discussing that fact with Viper."

"I ain't going nowhere with you two. Now, get the fuck out of here!"

"You know damn well we aren't leaving here without you."

When the guy on Danny's left took a charging step forward, Danny pulled the trigger, firing two shots and hitting the guy right in the chest. I held my breath as I watched the man flail backwards and hit the ground with a hard thud. The room fell silent as we all stood there in complete shock and horror. Unable to control myself, I mumbled, "Oh god, Danny ... What have you done?"

When he turned to look at me, the second man used the opportunity to lunge towards him, tackling him to the ground. The gun flew from his hand, and a fight ensued. While Danny tried to fight him off, he was no match for the tattooed angry beast, and it wasn't long before he was rendered completely helpless. Even after Danny quit fighting, the guy kept hitting him, over and over, and after one hard blow to the jaw, he was knocked unconscious. Fearing the guy might kill him, I rushed towards him, pushing him with all my might as I shouted, "Stop! Get the hell off him!"

"Holy shit!" The guy gave me a firm shove, forcing me off him. "Where the fuck did you come from?"

I should've been terrified of the guy. He was three times bigger than me with biceps the size of tree trunks, but I was too worried about my brother to care what he might do to me. I could almost feel the adrenaline surging through my veins as I lunged towards him once again and shouted, "Get off him!"

"Back the fuck off, lady."

"I will as soon as you leave him alone. He's already unconscious. If you don't stop, you'll kill him!"

"Would serve the motherfucker right." With that, the guy stood up, leaving Danny still sprawled out on the floor, unconscious. He was out cold, bruised and swollen, but I was relieved to see that he was still breathing. "There. I'm off the piece of shit. Happy now?"

"No, I'm far from happy," I grumbled as I glanced over at the man Danny had shot. "Doesn't look like your friend is all that happy either. You might want to call an ambulance or something before he bleeds out."

"Rafe!" I watched as he rushed over to the man. "You all right, brother?"

"Yeah, it's just a flesh wound," Rafe answered as he clung to his wounds.

"You sure about that? You're losing a lot of blood."

They both looked up at me like I'd lost my ever-loving mind when I stepped towards them and said, "Let me at least see what you're dealing with."

"Fuck that! You stand over there and keep your fucking mouth shut."

I should've done what he said, but Danny's life was on the line. If Rafe died, they would more than likely kill him or he could end up in jail for murder. Neither of those seemed like a good option, so I pushed, "I'm a nurse ... I can help if you let me."

"I told you to keep your fucking mouth shut!"

"Come on, Shotgun. Won't do any harm for her to have a look."

Rafe and Shotgun weren't your typical nicknames, but as I stood there watching the two men interact with one another, I realized there wasn't anything typical about either one of them. Shotgun looked far from pleased as he glanced over to me and ordered, "Fine, but make it fast."

Hearing his fierce tone made me regret my offer, but considering the present situation, I had no other choice. I went over and knelt down beside them, carefully lifting his t-shirt so I could get a better look at his injuries. While it looked pretty gruesome, the wound on his abdomen was just a deep graze, slicing the guy's flesh just above his hip with an angry black burn. The second bullet, on the other hand, had actually pierced through his upper chest next to his shoulder. Needing to get a better look, I asked, "Can you lean forward so I can see if there's an exit wound?"

Rafe nodded, then grimaced as he lifted himself up, giving me better access to his back. After just a few seconds, he asked, "How's it look?"

"You got lucky. The bullet went straight through, but you need to get to a hospital."

"Not a chance."

"What? Why not?"

"'Cause I fucking said so," he snapped.

"Fine. Do what you want, but we need to slow down this bleeding." I got up and rushed to the bathroom. After I grabbed a couple of towels, I hurried back into the living room and offered them to his friend. "Here, use these to apply pressure to the wounds."

Glaring at me like I'd been the one who'd pulled the trigger, he jerked the towels from my hand and placed them on Rafe's chest, doing his best to get the bleeding under control. "We need to get you back to the clubhouse. You think you can walk, or do you need me to—"

"I can walk, 'Gun," Rafe interrupted. "Just gonna need you to get me to my feet."

I watched silently as he helped Rafe up. Once he was standing, Shotgun turned his attention to Danny. He gave him a hard kick to the side as he growled, "Get up, asshole."

"Hey!" I scolded as I rushed over to Danny, shielding him with my body. "What's your problem?"

"And what the fuck is it to you?"

"He's my brother."

"Your brother?" he asked sounding surprised.

"Yes, my brother!" I looked down at Danny, giving him a gentle shake as I asked softly, "Hey ... Are you okay?"

Without giving him a chance to answer, Shotgun asked, "You got any idea what kind of trouble he's gotten himself into?"

"No, I have no idea, but I seriously doubt you killing each other is going to solve anything." I gave him another nudge as I pleaded, "Come on, Danny. Wake up."

His eyes finally fluttered open, and he groaned when he found me kneeling next to him. "You were supposed to stay in the bedroom, Delilah."

"Guess she didn't want to miss out on the party." Shotgun reached down and grabbed Danny by the arm, jerking him to his feet. He yanked his hands behind his back, and as he bound his wrists together with a zip-tie, he snarled, "Let's go, Danny boy. We have some business to tend to."

"Wait! You can't just take him like this. That's kidnapping!" I shouted. "I'll call the police and—"

"Hate to break it to you, sweet cheeks," Shotgun growled as he released Danny and grabbed me, pulling my arms behind my back and zip-tying my wrists together like he'd done Danny's, "but you're not calling anybody."

"What the hell do you think you're doing?" I barked.

"I'm taking you with us."

"The hell you say!" I jolted to the side, trying to break free from his grasp, but I simply wasn't strong enough. "Let me go or I'll scream!"

"We don't have time for this bullshit, 'Gun," Rafe groaned.

"Well, I can't just leave her here." He reached behind him and pulled out his gun, shoving it into my side as he ordered, "Move your ass, or I'll end you right here and now."

With his gun still pressed against my spine, I started out of the apartment, and Rafe and Danny followed us down the stairs. As we got closer to the parking lot, Danny leaned over to me and said, "You should've stayed in the bedroom."

"You should've kept your nose clean and not gotten involved with these hoodlums!" As the words left my mouth, I felt the barrel of the gun dig into my back. That should've been enough to make me shut up, but sadly, it wasn't. "How exactly are you involved with them? Is it drugs? Oh, my god, Danny. Please tell me you weren't stupid enough—"

"*Delilah ...*"

"And then you went and shot one of them! Seriously, Danny. What were you thinking?"

"Not exactly the best time to talk about it, Dee."

Shotgun lead us over to a black Ford pickup, then opened the door and shoved us inside. Once he'd closed the door, he went over and helped Rafe. While he was getting him settled, I looked back over to Danny and asked, "What are they going to do to us?"

"I don't know. You wouldn't even be tangled up in all this if you'd just—"

"Don't you dare try to twist this around on me. You're the one who made the decision to get involved in all this!" I shook my head as I asked, "You do realize that you could wind up in jail, right?"

"That's the least of my worries right now."

"Hmph. You're probably right." I huffed. "How could you do this, especially after all we went through as kids? You'd think—"

"Dammit, Delilah. I already told you! This isn't the time for this shit."

"When is the time, Danny? After these guys put a bullet in your head?"

Shotgun was just about to close the truck door when Rafe grumbled, "I can't take anymore, man. Can you do something to shut her up?"

"What?" My eyes widened with fear as Shotgun nodded and headed over to my side of the truck. When he opened the door, I shrieked, "I'll stop. I won't say another word. I swear!"

"Not buying that shit for a minute, sweetheart."

"No, seriously. I'll keep my mouth shut." When he reached behind me, I gasped. "Wait! What are you doing to do?"

He pulled out a roll of silver duct tape, and as he tore off a long strip, he announced, "I'm gonna give our ears a fucking break."

With that, he slapped the tape over my mouth and then got inside the truck. A million questions raced through my mind as I sat there bound and gagged. I had no idea where we were going as I stared out the window, praying that we'd crash or someone would see us and come to our rescue. Unfortunately, neither of those things happened. Instead, we pulled through a large metal gate with tall fencing surrounding what looked to be an old warehouse. There were guards standing at each entrance, giving me an uneasy feeling as the truck came to a stop at the front door. Rafe's focus was on that door as he muttered, "I'm good here for a minute. Take Danny in first."

Shotgun hesitated for a moment, but eventually nodded and got out of the truck. He went over to Danny's side and opened the door. With a quick jerk, he pulled him out and led him towards the front door. After shoving him inside, Shotgun disappeared, only to return moments later with two other men. It was dark, making it impossible to see what either of them looked like. Not that it mattered. Even when they opened the door and the light came on, none of them seemed to even notice that I was in the back. They were too busy trying to help Rafe out of the truck. As soon as they got him out, they all disappeared into the building. Several moments had passed, and I was beginning to think they'd forgotten about me, when I noticed the back door open. My heart started racing as I noticed a figure walking towards the truck. In a blink, the door opened, and the interior light flickered on, revealing the most incredibly handsome man I'd ever seen. He was tall and muscular with dark hair and fierce green eyes that seemed to pierce straight through me. I could tell by the vest he was wearing that he was one of them, so I expected him to yank me out of the truck and haul me inside like they'd done to Danny. He didn't. Instead, he just stood there staring at me.

Damn. I thought I was scared earlier, but something about the way he was looking at me brought butterflies to my stomach, and that completely terrified me.

HAWK

I was torn by my own ever-growing curiosity and the best course of action for handling the beautiful redhead I'd found sitting in the back of Shotgun's pickup. I wanted to take the tape from her mouth, ask her who she was, and how she was involved in all this mess with Danny, but something told me if I asked, I'd be climbing down a rabbit hole and never find my way out. Besides, with Rafe being shot and the club finally having our hands on Danny, I didn't have time to waste with some broad—no matter how beautiful she was. Having no other choice, I got her out of the truck and led her inside. Not knowing who she was made it difficult to know where to put her. I figured she couldn't do much damage bound and gagged, so I put her in one of the empty bedrooms with an exterior deadbolt to lock her inside. Just before I walked out, I stopped to study her for a moment. As I stood there looking at the beautiful creature, I considered removing the tape from her mouth, but then, I noticed the way she was glaring at me—like she wanted to scream for help or slit my throat—so I decided against it. Instead, I simply walked out of the room and closed the door.

Once I had her locked inside, I went down to our makeshift infirmary to check in on Rafe. When I walked in, Shotgun and Viper were hovering over the gurney as Doc assessed Rafe's condition. Just as I was walking up, I heard Doc tell Rafe, "You got lucky, brother. Real lucky."

"Don't feel all that lucky at the moment," Rafe complained.

"Well, you're lucky nonetheless," Doc replied. "I'm surprised he didn't do more damage at such close range."

"The piece of shit was a lousy shot," Rafe grumbled.

"Clearly."

While I was pleased to hear that Rafe was going to be okay, I was curious to know how he had ended up getting shot. I was about to ask when Viper beat me to it. "So, what the hell happened?"

"Things got out of hand," Shotgun started. "We tried telling Danny that we needed to talk to him, but he wasn't having it. Without any explanation, he told us to get the fuck out, and when we didn't, he drew his pistol. I thought he was bullshittin'. I never thought the dumbass would have the balls to actually pull the fucking trigger."

"Neither of us did," Rafe admitted. "Guess he felt backed into a corner and decided to take his fucking chances."

"That's a mistake he'll soon regret," Viper snarled. "But first, we're gonna need him to talk. It's the only way we're ever gonna know what the hell happened with that last shipment."

"If he knows anything, I'll get it out of him," Shotgun assured us.

"Good. I'm counting on you to do just that. Menace took him down to your holding room."

"I'm on it."

When he started towards the door, I asked, "Hold up ... What's the deal with the girl?"

"Damn. I almost forgot about her." Shotgun turned back to us with a shrug. "She's his sister or something. Got the feeling she didn't know anything about what Danny was up to."

"Then, why'd you bring her back here?"

"The way she was running her fucking mouth, there was no way we could've left her behind."

"What was she running her mouth about?"

"*Everything*... Us being there. Me being shot. Danny getting himself into trouble. You name it. The girl was downright pissed." Rafe chuckled as he added, "Fuck. She was giving Danny hell up one side and down the other. You should've heard her. It got so bad I almost started feeling sorry for the guy, and that's saying something."

"That why you taped her mouth shut?"

"Hell, yeah," Shotgun answered. "Couldn't take another minute of her yammering on."

"So, what are we going to do with her now?"

"Got no idea," Shotgun answered. "Probably would've left her if she hadn't threatened to go to the fucking cops. At least now we know she isn't gonna have them sniffing around and asking questions we don't wanna answer."

"He's got a point there," Rafe replied. "Talk to her. You'll see for yourself why we didn't leave her behind."

"Where is she?" Viper asked.

"I locked her inside the empty room next to Bear's," I answered.

"Good." Viper turned to Shotgun. "You go deal with Danny and see what you can find out. Hawk and I will talk to the girl."

"You got it."

When Shotgun headed towards the door, Viper turned his attention to Doc. "Take care of our boy. I'll be back later to check on him."

Doc nodded, then Viper and I left the room to go talk to the spitfire. As we walked down the hall, I found myself thinking about the moment I'd opened the truck door and found her sitting inside. Everything about her, from the intense look in her eyes to the blue nursing scrubs she was wearing, intrigued me. The revelation seemed odd to me. I wasn't a man who was usually so captivated by a woman, especially one who hadn't even spoken, but there was something about her that interested me, and I was eager to find out everything there was to know about her. After I unlocked the door, I followed Viper inside, and we found her sitting on the edge of the bed—hands still bound behind her, but the tape was starting to curl around the edges where she'd been trying to remove it.

Viper stepped over and crouched down in front of her. She never moved a muscle as he looked her dead in the eyes and said, "I'm Viper, and this is Hawk."

Her eyes skirted over to me for a split second. Then her attention went back to Viper as he told her, "We have some questions for you. I figure we've got two ways we can go about it—the easy way and *the hard way*. Personally, I'd just as soon go about this the easy way. How about you?"

She nodded in agreement.

"Good." As he reached for the duct tape, he told her, "I'm gonna remove this, but don't make me regret it."

After he carefully pulled the tape from her mouth, he stood up, towering over her. "You got a name?"

"Delilah."

"Okay, Delilah. You gonna behave if I remove those restraints?"

"Yes." With his pocket knife in hand, Viper reached around her, and the second he sliced the plastic, freeing her wrists, Delilah asked, "Where's Danny?"

"Oh no, sweetheart," he growled. "I'm the one asking the questions."

"And I'll try and answer them." Without showing any sign of fear, she held Viper's gaze. "I just want to know if my brother's okay."

"Damn, Rafe was right. You are a feisty one," Viper grumbled as he shook his head. He was clearly as surprised as I was that the girl didn't seem the least bit shaken by the situation she'd found herself in. Hell, even I would've been a little unnerved if I was in her shoes, but she came off cool, calm, and collected. She was either one hell of an actress, or she was too fucking pissed to realize that her life was on the line. A part of me wanted to warn her, to tell her that we were the kind of men who wouldn't think twice about putting a bullet in her head, but before I got the chance, Viper looked down at her and said, "Danny's alive ... at least he is for now. That could change for you both if you two don't give us the answers we're looking for."

She flinched slightly at his response, then let out a deep, aggravated breath. "Then we have a problem."

"And what's that?"

"I don't know anything about what Danny's done or why we're here."

"Don't tell me you really expect me to believe that shit."

"I don't have a death wish, and I don't want anything to happen to my brother, so there's no reason for me to lie to you," she snapped back. "It might be hard to believe, but I'm telling you the truth."

"Okay, I'm gonna just assume for the time being that you are actually telling the truth, and you don't know anything about what your brother was up to." Viper crossed his arms. "Let's try to figure out what you do know. Where are you both from?"

"Here in Tennessee ... about thirty-five minutes away. A small town called LaGrange. We moved there about fifteen or so years ago."

"What about your folks? Where are they?"

"My mom still lives in LaGrange. I don't know about my father." She shrugged as she continued, "I haven't seen him since my mother left him."

"What about friends? Does Danny have anyone in particular he hangs with?"

"I don't know. At one time, he had a few guys he ran around with, but honestly, I'm not sure if he still talks to them anymore."

"Does he leave town a lot?"

"Danny's almost thirty years old. He doesn't exactly check in with me to let me know when he's coming or going."

"What about a job?"

"If I had to guess, I'd say he doesn't have one, but I really can't say for sure."

"You don't know anything about who his handler is or where we might find them?"

"Handler? I'm sorry, but I have no idea what you're talking about." Her expression softened as she lowered her head and explained, "I know it sounds bad that I don't know more about what's going on with my brother right now. I love him dearly, and I'd do anything I could to help him, but I don't know every detail of his life. If I did, I'd tell you."

Viper didn't respond. Instead, he simply stood there, studying her as he tried to determine if she was telling the truth. After several moments, she glanced up at Viper with tear-filled eyes and asked, "What's this all about? What's a handler? Is it drugs ... or something else?"

"Best if we keep that under wraps for now."

Her voice trembled when she asked him, "Are you going to hurt him?"

"That'll be up to him," Viper answered honestly. "Actually, that goes for the both of you."

Her beautiful blue eyes widened with panic as the severity of the situation started to sink in. Involved or not, her life was on the line, and depending on how things turned out with Danny, there was a chance she wouldn't make it out alive. That was a realization that didn't sit well with either her or me. Her lip quivered as she asked, "You aren't going to let me go?"

"Sorry, doll, but that's not an option."

"But I have a job. People are depending on me. If I'm not there, then they'll—"

"They'll manage," Viper interrupted. "They have no other choice."

"So, what? You're just going to keep me locked up in this room?"

"As a matter of fact, that's exactly what we're going to do." Viper surprised us both when he turned his attention to me and said, "I'm trusting you to keep an eye on her. She doesn't leave this room without you by her side, and she doesn't leave the clubhouse. If she gives you any trouble, put a bullet in her."

"Understood."

Normally, I had no problem being alone with a beautiful woman, but I was suddenly filled with pure and utter dread as I watched Viper walk out of the room and close the door behind him. I glanced over at Delilah, still sitting on the edge of the bed, and when her eyes met mine, a feeling of unease washed over me. It wasn't anything she'd said or done. It was simply the way I felt standing in that room with her—like I wanted to toss that hot little body of hers across the bed and fuck her senseless—that had me on edge. Viper had put me in charge of watching over her, and I had every intention of doing the job I was ordered to do—nothing more, nothing less. With her eyebrows furrowed and her lips pursed in disgust, Delilah glared back at me and asked, "Are you just going to stand there and stare at me?"

"Do you always just say whatever's on your mind?"

"Yeah ... I guess I do." A light scoff slipped through her lips. "I should probably work on that."

My words dripped with sarcasm as I replied, "Yeah, might be a good idea."

She studied my cut for a moment, then asked, "So, who are you guys anyway?"

"Who we are isn't important."

"Then, it shouldn't be a big deal to tell me who you are," she sassed. "Besides, it's not like I can't read. You all have the name Ruthless Sinners on your vests. Are you a gang or something?"

I glanced over at the duct tape Viper had removed from her and growled, "You know, you're really tempting me to put that tape back on your mouth."

"You wouldn't."

"You don't think so?" I held her gaze. "Try me."

DELILAH

I didn't know what had gotten into me. I should've been scared out of my mind when Viper and Hawk came into the room to question me, but it was like that part of my brain simply wasn't working how it was supposed to. I wanted to think it was just all the anger and frustration pumping through my veins that was making it difficult to see that my life was in danger, but I knew that wasn't the only reason I wasn't thinking clearly. It was him—the handsome stranger who brought butterflies to my stomach every time he looked at me. I didn't know what was wrong with me. I was a smart girl. I knew Hawk was one of *them*—the men who'd threatened my brother's life and my own. For that matter, he was the one who'd brought me into this godforsaken room and locked me inside, yet I still found him to be irresistibly, earth-shatteringly hot. Every time I looked at his broad, muscular shoulders, dark tousled hair, and piercing green eyes, my pulse would start to race, and my entire body would grow warm with desire. It was bad to even give a man like him a second look. I knew that. Regrettably, I couldn't seem to make my body understand that. I needed to get as far away from him as possible. Unfortunately, that wasn't going to happen. Because of Danny, I was stuck there with him, and if I wasn't careful and didn't stay out of trouble, he'd end me once and for all. Damn. I was screwed.

"Fine ... I'm *sorry*." Trying my best to sound sincere, I glanced up at him and added, "I won't say another word."

"Yeah, somehow I find that hard to believe."

His eyes met mine, and an unwelcome shiver traveled down my spine, forcing me to quickly look away. My eyes drifted to the floor, and as I sat there studying the scuff marks on my tennis shoes, I found myself wishing I'd changed out of my work clothes and into something else —*anything else*. Maybe then it wouldn't bother me so much that I could feel him staring at me. When I couldn't stand it a moment longer, I shifted, positioning myself so that my back was to him. I crossed my legs and toyed with my fingernails, trying to pretend that he was no longer in the room. I'd never been good at being quiet, much less still, so I quickly became uncomfortable. The silence in the room wasn't making it any easier, and my leg started to lightly bounce up and down. I let out a deep breath and tried counting the tiles on the ceiling, but I just couldn't keep my focus. When I couldn't stand it a moment longer, I glanced over my shoulder, and just as I feared, Hawk was staring right at me. A knowing smirk crossed his face.

"You just can't stand it, can you?"

"What? I didn't say anything."

"Yeah, and it's eating at ya something awful."

"No, it's not!"

"*Yeah.* Sure, it's not." He shook his head as he snickered. "Looks like you're about to come out of your skin over there."

I rolled my eyes as I positioned my hips even further to the left, making it even more difficult for him to see my face. "I'm just fine, *thank you very much.*"

"Um-hmm."

My back was still to him when I heard him move behind me, but I refused to turn and look. Instead, I just sat there as still as possible, glaring at the blank wall in front of me. I remained that way even after I heard the door open and close. I thought he was just messing with me until I heard the click of the exterior lock—that was one sound I couldn't ignore. I quickly turned around and was surprised to see that there was no sign of Hawk. Still not believing he was truly gone, I got up and walked over to the door, testing it to see if it was really locked. When I felt that it was, I decided to use the moment alone to check out my surroundings. I went over to the window, quickly testing it to see if I could get it open; when I couldn't, I tried the window in the bathroom. After seeing that it wouldn't budge either, I rushed over to the dresser and searched through the drawers, but they were all empty. I stood in the center of the small room, searching for anything that might help me out of my precarious situation and was disappointed when there was nothing to be found. Having no other choice, I walked back over to the bed and lay down.

I hadn't realized how exhausted I was until I rested my head down on the pillow. There was no way I could actually sleep. I was too worried about Danny for that to happen. Those men had him somewhere in this building, and they were doing god knows what to him for god knows why. It was a thought that terrified me and made me even more curious about what he'd gotten himself into. The Danny I knew, the brother I'd grown up with and loved so dearly, was now a stranger to me, and it was all my fault. I was too wrapped up in my own life, too busy being focused on my career to think about Danny and what he was going through. I should've done better. I should've called more, gone to see him—been more involved in his life. Maybe then, he wouldn't have found himself in such a terrible predicament. I was wallowing in a pit of self-loathing when the door opened and Hawk appeared with a tray of food and a handful of clothes. I sat up in the bed and watched silently as he walked over to the corner and placed them on the desk. "I thought you might be hungry."

"Oh?" I was surprised by the gesture, especially after the way he'd just up and left, so I was a little hesitant as I got up and muttered, "Well, umm ... thank you."

"No problem." He motioned his hand towards the pile of clothes and announced, "I also got you a change of clothes."

"Okay." I got up and walked over to him, looking at all the things he'd brought. While I should've been grateful that he'd even thought to bring me anything, I wasn't. "So, where did these come from?"

"They're just some clothes. Why does it matter?"

"Well, it might not matter to you, but it does to me." He didn't respond. Instead, he just stood there looking at me like I was being a complete bitch. I couldn't blame him. I *was* being a bitch, but I didn't know what kind of women he ran around with. If I had to guess, they were nothing like me—average looking with a boring life and limited experience with men. A part of me was unsettled by that fact. To be honest, I was more than unsettled. For reasons I didn't understand, I was actually feeling jealous. I just couldn't get a grip on my green-eyed monster and found myself crossing my arms as I looked over to him with a scowl. "I don't want to catch something from one of your little bimbos that won't wash off."

"Bimbos? Are you fucking kidding?" With a snarl on his face, he picked up one of the t-shirts and held it out to me. "These are brand new. Hell, they still have the fucking tags on them."

"Oh ... I missed that." A sudden feeling of guilt washed over me, and I wished I could take back what I'd said. It wasn't like me to be so catty. I was normally a pretty nice person who was respectful and kind. Nothing like I'd been behaving. I lowered my head and whispered, "I'm ... I'm sorry. I didn't realize."

"Um-hmm." I would've given anything to read his mind as he stood there silently studying me with narrowed eyes. His back was stiff, his jaw was locked, and he looked like there was a storm raging inside of him. If I wasn't careful, I was going to make an even bigger mess of this whole thing. After several long, agonizing minutes, he finally ran his hand over his face and sighed. "You know, I'm not the bad guy here."

"Are you sure about that?" I asked as I turned and went over to sit on the edge of the bed. "You are the one in charge of keeping me here. I also recall hearing that you should put a bullet in my head if I cause any trouble."

"Maybe, but you gotta remember, I wouldn't have been told to keep an eye on you if your brother hadn't—"

"Hadn't what?" I pushed. "What did he do?"

"It's not important."

"We both know that's not true; otherwise, you wouldn't be keeping me here." I looked over to him and softened my tone as I said, "I just don't get why you won't tell me what's going on. I deserve to know why I'm being forced to stay. I deserve to know what my brother has done."

"I don't disagree." He ran his hand through his tousled hair and sighed. "But the decision isn't up to me. If Viper wanted you to know, he'd tell you."

"Okay ... so, who is this Viper guy anyway?"

"He's the president."

"President? President of what … the Ruthless Sinners?"

"That's right," he admitted. "He's the one in charge, so do us both a favor and don't get on his bad side."

I thought back to our earlier conversation—the tone in his voice, the tone in mine—and groaned. "I'm afraid it's a little late for that."

"It's never too late, Delilah. Just do what you can to keep it together until we figure this thing out with your brother."

"Okay."

I had no idea how I was supposed to keep it together when there were so many things I simply didn't understand—why I was even there, what Danny had done, or why I continued to feel such a pull towards Hawk when I should've wanted to run as far away from him as possible. I suddenly felt like the walls were closing in on me, and even though I'd tried to fight it, I felt tears begin to sting my eyes. A strange look crossed Hawk's face as he took a step towards me. I stood frozen as he lifted his hand to my face, gently brushing the pad of his thumb across my cheek as he whispered, "It's going to be okay, Delilah."

"You don't know that for certain."

"No, but I'll do whatever I can to help ... to get you back home where you belong."

"Why do you care what happens to me anyway?"

He took a step back as he removed his hand from my face. "Because I believe you when you say you weren't involved in this."

"Oh, well ... um ... if that's the case, can I ask you something?"

"You can ask. Doesn't mean I'll answer."

"Is Danny okay? Have you hurt him?" His face twisted into a grimace, and I knew I had my answer. Danny might be alive, but he definitely wasn't okay. I dropped my head into the palms of my hands as I cried, "Oh, god. This is bad. Really bad. I should've done something."

"What could you have done?"

"I don't know ... *something*." I lowered my hands and started pacing back and forth. "He's my brother. I should've at least known he was in trouble. Maybe then I could've helped him in some way."

"If everything you've said is true and you had no part in it, then none of this is your fault. Your brother is a big boy. He can take responsibility for his own shit. He doesn't need you to do it for him."

"It's not that simple. He's my family, Hawk. It doesn't matter what he did or didn't do. I'm supposed to be there for him, have his back, and stand by him when things are tough, and I failed him." I had to bite back my tears. "I want him to be okay ... I need him to be okay."

"I can't make any promises about Danny, Delilah. I wish I could, but it's out of my hands."

"What about me?" I knew I couldn't do anything to help my brother while I was locked up in this room. I needed to get out, find some answers to what was going on, and then, maybe—just maybe, I might be able to help him get out of this mess. "Do you think there's any way I'll be able to get out of here?"

"I can't say for sure." He shrugged. "That depends on your brother."

"If I could talk to him, then maybe—"

"That's not going to happen." He glanced over at the clock. "I've gotta get going. Watch some TV, sleep, or something. Just try to stay out of trouble until I get back."

"Okay ... I'll try."

Hawk's lips twitched into a smile, almost knocking me off my feet, and then he headed for the door. I watched him walk out of the room and close the door, leaving me alone once again. Even though he got under my skin and had a way of making me act like a complete asshole, I was actually a little sad to see him go. I didn't want to obsess over the fact that I was locked in a room alone, so I grabbed a few of the clothes Hawk had brought me and went into the bathroom for a shower. Once I was done, I put on a t-shirt with a pair of knit leggings, surprised to find that they fit perfectly. I used the hairdryer stashed in the bathroom cabinet, then grabbed a pack of crackers and a drink before climbing back in bed. Even though I wasn't in the mood to watch anything, I turned on the TV and sat there listening to one of those infomercials on some new cooking device while I ate. Needless to say, it wasn't the most entertaining night, so I gave into my exhaustion and nestled into bed.

I closed my eyes, but instead of drifting off to sleep, I thought about Danny and what they might be doing to him. I wanted to think that they were just talking to him, but I knew better. Men like the Ruthless Sinners weren't about talking. They were about getting results—by any means necessary. My imagination started to run wild with horrific thoughts. I hated the idea of my brother being hurt. I hated the idea of him dying even more. With all the crazy notions whipping around in my head, I feared I'd never manage to fall asleep. Thankfully, after several hours of relentless crying and praying, I finally drifted off—unaware of the fact that my life was about to change in ways I couldn't comprehend.

HAWK

"I'm telling you ... I didn't have anything to do with it," Danny's hands were bound over his head, his face black and blue with bruises, and his eyes were almost swollen shut. Shotgun had been doing a real number on him, but Danny still hadn't fessed up to a damn thing. "I swear it."

"I'm not buying your bullshit. Not for a goddamn second," Shotgun growled. "The brothers have been over to your place. We know you were packing up your shit. It's time for you to explain where you were going and why."

"I ... uh ..."

Shotgun reached up and grabbed him by the throat, squeezing tightly as he snarled, "Think before you speak, Danny. Any more bullshit and I'm going to break out my tools, and trust me, you don't want that to happen."

"You're right. I was getting out of town."

"Why?"

"I ... um ... had to go out on a run."

Anyone in that room could see he was lying, especially Shotgun. With an angry scowl, he walked over to the counter and picked up an ice pick, then carried it back over to Danny and quickly stabbed it into his outer thigh. Writhing around like a worm on a hook, Danny wailed out a stream of curses. Once he started to settle down, Shotgun growled, "What don't you get, Danny? I already told you that I'm done with the bullshit. Where were you going?"

"I-I was gettin'... out of town," he stammered.

"Why?"

"'Cause I had to."

"Why?"

Shotgun waited for Danny to respond. When he didn't, he walked back over and grabbed another ice pick. His swollen eyes widened as he watched Shotgun saunter back over to him, then he started to squirm and plead, "Wait. Wait! Please don't."

Showing no signs of hesitation, Shotgun took the ice pick and slammed it into Danny's other thigh, causing him to once again bellow out with anguish. As I stood there watching the scene unfold before me, I couldn't understand why Danny was being so fucking stubborn. He was only making it harder on himself by holding out. Shotgun ground the ice pick further into his flesh as he warned, "Don't make me ask again."

"I found out ... that the coke I gave ... you was counterfeit." He heavily panted. "I knew you'd come after me ... so I was gonna skip town before that happened."

"You found out?" Shotgun grumbled. "You saying you didn't know it was counterfeit all along?"

"Had no idea until I got the call."

"What call?"

"A friend tipped me off ... told me everything was fucked up with the last take."

"What friend?" Shotgun pushed.

He hesitated for a moment, but the second Shotgun started to turn towards his tools, Danny mumbled, "It was Tracy ... Tracy Earnhardt." When Shotgun didn't respond, he continued, "You know ... 'Starlight' from the strip club."

Shotgun glanced over his shoulder at Viper and me, and there was no missing the anger in his eyes. Tracy had been working at Stilettoes for over a year, and we'd always thought she was one of our best girls. As far as we knew, she was a good kid, always on time and did as she was told, so hearing that she'd been running her mouth was difficult for both of us to digest. "You telling me that Starlight called you and warned you about the coke being counterfeit?"

"Yeah. She was worried you guys would think it was me who fucked with the product. But it wasn't me, I swear it!"

Shotgun took a step back and glared at Danny, mulling over everything he'd admitted. "So, I'm supposed to believe that when you delivered our two hundred grand worth of product that you didn't have any idea it'd been fucked with?"

"Look, I know it might be hard to believe, but I didn't know shit about it. I just did what I always do. I placed the order and went to pick it up." Danny actually sounded sincere as he continued, "I ain't stupid. I've been working with you guys long enough to know what you'd do to me if I tried to pull some fucked-up shit like that. Besides, you guys tested the shit, same as I did. You saw for yourselves that it was the same as always."

Viper stepped forward and asked, "Which brother tested it?"

"The guy who came to my place. The one I shot. He tried it out and said we were cool."

"He's right," Shotgun replied. "But he didn't test each bag. With the size take we had, there was no way we could test it all."

"I'm telling ya, what I tested was good. I assumed it was all good." Danny repeated once again, "I'm telling ya, it wasn't me who did this shit."

"If it wasn't you, then who was it?"

"I got no idea. Maybe it was somebody on your end." Shotgun started towards his tools, this time grabbing his blowtorch and carrying it back over to Danny. "Easy man ... I didn't mean that shit. Maybe it was my handler or even the man at the top. I don't know. I'm just the go-between. They don't tell me nothing."

"Who's your handler?"

"I don't know nothing about him. Just that he goes by the name Miller. I meet up with him in Pine Bluff when I need to pick up a shipment." Blood trickled down from his lip as he spoke. "I just text what I need and meet him a day later with the cash."

Danny had barely gotten the words out of his mouth when Viper stepped forward and asked, "The number still on your phone?"

"Yeah," Danny answered. "Last time I used it was when I made arrangements to pick up your take."

Viper turned to Shotgun and me and nodded his head, signaling us to follow him out of the room. Once the door closed behind us, he turned to me and said, "Get the phone to Menace. Have him track the number and see if he can find out anything about this guy Miller or their main supplier. We need to know exactly who the fuck we're dealing with."

"You got it."

"It's late. Let's call it a night. We can get back at it early tomorrow morning."

I could tell by Shotgun's expression that he wasn't ready to stop. He was finally making some headway with Danny, but he'd never go against orders. "You want me to let him down or leave him strung up for the night?"

"Leave him. It'll give him some time to think things over before we start in on him again."

"Understood."

Once we'd retrieved the cellphone from Danny, Viper and Shotgun headed out, while I took the phone to Menace. After I gave him the rundown of what we needed, I went to check in on Delilah. It was late, and just as I'd expected, when I opened the door, she was sound asleep. Deciding it was best to let her get some shuteye, I closed the door and went to the room across the hall. I hoped by staying there I could keep a closer eye on her. Besides, I was too fucking exhausted to go back to my place, so I left the door open and collapsed on the bed. As I lay there, I thought back to my earlier conversation with Delilah. Hearing her talk about being there for her brother got to me. Delilah didn't care if her brother was in the wrong or that he should take the responsibility for his own actions, she wanted to support him just the same. It was rare to find an outsider who held the same beliefs about loyalty and family as my brothers and me. Our whole life was driven by the brotherhood, always having each other's backs and being there for one another when times were rough. It had me wondering if there were other things we had in common. With each moment I thought about it, I found myself becoming more and more exhausted. I could barely remember closing my eyes when I was jerked awake by the sound of Axel's voice saying, "Hey, brother. Viper's called us in."

As I sat up and wiped the sleep from my eyes, I asked, "What time is it?"

"Just after six."

"All right. I'll be right there."

He nodded, then disappeared into the hallway. I pulled myself out of bed, and after a quick run to the bathroom, I went to check in on Delilah. Not wanting to just barge in on her, I tapped on the door as I unlocked it. When I stepped inside, I found her still in bed watching TV. When I glanced over at the screen, I was surprised to see she was watching *Animal Kingdom*—one of my favorite shows. I'd stumbled across the series a few months back when I was nursing a hell of a hangover and quickly became engrossed in the crazy family. The three sons and their lunatic mother were always into something, and I found it hard to believe that a woman like Delilah would be interested in all of their antics. She drew me from my thoughts as she sat up and turned off the TV. "Any news on Danny? Did you find out what you needed to know? Can I go home now?"

"Slow down, Delilah. As of now, nothing's changed."

"How long is this going to take?"

"Already told you ... That's up to Danny."

Worry filled her eyes as she asked, "So, he's ... still alive?"

"He is."

"Thank god."

It was clear Delilah was relieved that her brother was still alive, but her face was still marked with worry. I couldn't blame her. She was stuck in the middle of an impossible situation. Hoping to take her mind off things for a moment, I asked, "You a fan of *Animal Kingdom*?"

"Yeah, I guess." She cocked her head with curiosity. "Why? Do you watch it?"

"From time to time. Smurf is something else, isn't she?"

"She's a nutjob, but she makes the show."

"That she does." As I started out the door, I told her, "I've gotta get going. I'll be back in a few hours."

"Okay." She nodded, and just as I was about to close the door, she asked, "Hey, do you think I might be able to make a call into work? I need to let them know I won't be coming in."

"Doubt Viper will go for that."

"It's not like me to just not show up for work," she pushed. "I doubt anyone but my mother would notice that Danny's not around, but if I don't at least text my lead nurse, they'll get suspicious and—"

"I'll talk to Viper and let you know."

"Okay, but my shift starts in a couple of hours and—"

"I said I'd talk to him, Delilah."

With a look of defeat, she sighed. "Okay."

"I'll be back when I can."

With that, I closed the door and went down to the conference room to join Viper and the others. When I walked in, they were already seated and waiting for me to do the same. As soon as I was settled, Viper announced, "You all know that we brought Danny in last night, and he spent some quality time with Shotgun. I'd like to say that we got everything sorted and this thing with him is done, but unfortunately that isn't the case."

"So, what's going on?" Axel asked. "Who fucked us over?"

"Can't say for sure ... at least, not yet." Viper turned to Menace and asked, "What were you able to find out?"

"Don't have a lot just yet, but I'm still working on it." He took a piece of paper out of his file and handed it over to Viper. "Lives in Texarkana. From what I can tell, he's just another go-between. I tracked the burner he was using, and it looks like he goes to Texas at least once a week, if not more."

"Got a name?"

"Not yet."

"Is he making drug runs to Texas?" I asked.

"That would make sense, but I can't be certain just yet."

As Axel looked over at the paper Menace had given Viper, he said, "Not much here. Looks like you have your work cut out for ya."

"I do, but I'll get it." He turned to Shotgun. "Need you to see if Danny knows anything more. Might help to know how he got his start dealing with these guys."

"No problem. I'll get him talking."

"I have no doubt you will," Menace replied. "Since we have the sister, might be a good idea to have a chat with her as well."

My stomach twisted into a knot, and I couldn't stop

myself from saying, "We've already talked to her. It's pretty clear that she doesn't know anything."

Viper cocked his eyebrow as he told me, "We don't know that for certain."

"No, but my gut tells me she's speakin' the truth." I glanced around the room, and it was clear from their expressions that my brothers were surprised by my declaration. Hoping to play it off, I shrugged and said, "I don't see any reason for her to lie ... not when she's got nothing to gain and everything to lose."

"You might be right, but we'll never know unless Shotgun has a go with her."

As if he could sense my unease, Shotgun leaned forward and said, "Let me see what I can get out of Danny first. If he gives us what we need, there'll be no reason to involve the girl."

"He may have a point there. No need involving her any more than we have to. Otherwise, we'll just have another problem to contend with," Axel added.

The second the words came out of Axel's mouth Billy the Butcher came to my mind. He was the club's "cleaner." Whenever we had a mess to be cleaned up or a captive that needed to be dealt with, he would take care of it—using any means necessary. The thought of him handling Delilah made my blood run cold. I didn't get why it even bothered me. I knew nothing about her. It shouldn't have mattered to me what the brothers did or didn't do to her. Since she was already the topic of conversation, I decided to use the opportunity to say, "We've got another issue with the girl that needs to be considered."

"Oh?" Viper's brows furrowed as he asked, "And what's that?"

"She's got friends ... people she works with who'll be curious to know why she hasn't shown up to work. We don't want folks snooping around and trying to find her, so it might be best to let her contact someone ... make up a reason for being out of touch."

"Get her phone from Shotgun. You send the messages that need to be sent."

I nodded, and was relieved when the topic of Delilah quickly changed as Bear asked, "Any word on Rafe? I haven't had a chance to get down to the infirmary yet. He making it okay?"

"Yeah," Viper answered. "He's on the mend. Should be back on his feet in a couple of days."

"Good." His expression grew fierce as he added, "Hope Shotgun is giving Danny hell for putting a bullet in our brother."

"Don't worry. Danny is getting what's coming to him," Viper assured him as he leaned back in his chair and crossed his arms. "Two hundred grand is a lot of cash. I know you're all as eager as I am to get this thing dealt with ... and we will, but I don't want it distracting us from the bigger picture. We've got some leads on a new distributor that we'll be checking out, and we still have the new club to get up and running."

"I'll be heading over there this morning," Axel replied. "I want to see if those building permits have cleared so we can get going on the expansion."

"Good. I'll check on the liquor license and see if Cassandra has made any progress with getting us some new girls." Viper stood as he ordered, "The clock is ticking. Let's get this day rolling."

As we all started to disperse, Shotgun followed me out

the door and into the hall. A look of concern crossed his face as he asked, "Something going on with you that I need to be aware of?"

"No. Everything's good."

"You sure?" he pushed. "Sure seems like something is up with you and that girl."

"You talking about Delilah?" When he just stood there glaring at me, I shook my head. "No, brother. Nothing's up with her. Just want us to be careful."

"Oh, come on, man." A smirk crossed his face as he gave my shoulder a brotherly slap. "I'm just fucking with you. I know you're smarter than that."

He was right. I was smarter than that. It was time for me to get my head fucking sorted before I ended up doing something I'd regret. The thought had me thinking about Lisa's offer from the night before. I wanted to believe that some quality time with her might put an end to the nagging pull I'd felt towards Delilah, but I knew that wasn't the case. Nothing was going to get that woman out of my fucking head. When Shotgun started down the hall, I shouted, "I've got some shit to take care of. I'll be down in a bit to check your progress with Danny."

"See ya then."

As soon as he was out of sight, I went down to the kitchen. After I grabbed a cup of coffee and some biscuits, I headed to the room where we were holding Delilah. Once I'd unlocked the door, I walked in without saying a word and placed everything on the desk. She was still sitting on the bed and *Animal Kingdom* was back on the TV, but her eyes were trained solely on me as I turned and started back out the door. "That's it? You're just gonna leave without saying anything?"

"Nothing else to say."

"Seriously? I've been locked up in this room for hours on end, and you still aren't even going to tell me what the hell is going on?"

I turned to look at her, and the second her blue eyes locked on mine, I knew I'd made a mistake. She looked so fucking beautiful with her long red hair flowing down around her delicate shoulders, and just like that, she had me thinking things I had no business thinking. Fuck. I needed to get the hell out of there. "I don't have time for this shit, Delilah."

I stepped out into the hall, quickly closing the door behind me and locking it. Just before I turned to leave, I heard her bang on the door and shout, "Hawk. Hawk! You can't leave me in here like this!"

My chest tightened at the sound of her cries, but after meeting with the brothers, I knew she was safer in that room than she was anywhere else.

DELILAH

The haze of adrenaline and anger had officially worn off, and I was starting to freak out. My mind was reeling with unimaginable thoughts, and with every second that passed, I felt more and more like the walls were closing in on me, smothering my every breath. I was hoping for some small reprieve when Hawk came into the room with some coffee and breakfast, but instead, he only made matters worse. He barely spoke, and when he did, it was clear that he was on edge. I had no idea what had caused his change in demeanor, but it was impossible not to take it as a bad sign. I tried to settle my nerves by watching some TV as I drank my coffee. Unfortunately, I couldn't stay focused long enough to comprehend what was going on. My mind kept wandering to Danny and then to my mother and then to work. I had no doubt that Janet was going to be furious with me for not touching base and letting her know I wouldn't be coming in. I liked my job and the people I worked with, and I hated the thought of losing everything

I'd worked for because of something Danny had done. I'd like to say that things had gotten better over the next few hours, but they didn't. With every hour that dragged by, I found myself glancing over to the door, hoping by some chance that Hawk would return and allow me to call into work.

When I finally heard the click of the lock, I got up, anxiously waiting for him to enter the room, but he didn't. Instead of Hawk, a different guy—a much scarier, more intimidating man—stepped into the room. He had long dark hair and tattoos all over his arms up to his neck. His eyes were dark and cold as he charged into the room with a handful of drinks and a sack of food. I shifted to the corner of the room as I quietly asked, "Who are you?"

He placed the drinks and a bag of food on the desk. "Widow."

"I thought Hawk was supposed to be watching over me."

"He sent me."

"Oh, did he mention anything about me getting in touch with my work?"

"Nope."

"So, he didn't say anything?"

"Nope."

Without another word, he stalked out of the room, closed the door, and locked it behind him. Damn. I wanted to bang on the door, scream and shout for them to let me out, but something told me it was best for me to just keep my mouth shut. Feeling utterly defeated, I walked over to the desk, grabbed a bottle of water and a sandwich, then sat down on the edge of the bed. I started to take a bite of food, but with the panic that was building inside the pit of my stomach, I simply couldn't eat. Looking for something to unlock the door, I decided to check the desk again, and found a small hairpin in the side drawer. I held it in my hand and wondered if it would be possible for me to pick the door's lock. I'd never actually done it, but I figured it couldn't hurt to at least try. Even though I was eager to get started, I decided it was best to wait until dark. I quickly slipped the pin back into the drawer, and for the first time since I'd been taken captive, I felt hopeful that I might actually get out of here alive.

I went over to the bed, and as I lay down, I started trying to devise a plan. I thought back to the night before when I was brought to the warehouse and tried to remember every detail of what I'd seen: the long, dark hall; the bar with the jukebox and pool tables; the parking lot with the guards posted by the tall fence and gate. Damn. It seemed as if these men were prepared for anything. Even if I managed to pick the stupid lock, my escape wouldn't come easy. Every move I made would have to be well-thought-out, but I wasn't going to let it deter me from trying.

Hours later, I was still mulling over my plan when I heard the lock on the door turn. Moments later, Hawk stepped into the room and closed the door behind him. As I looked up at him, a warmth washed over me, and I silently cursed myself for my body's reaction to him. After the way he'd locked me in this godforsaken room, I should've been disgusted by him—angered at the very least. I hoped to hide my unwelcome reaction by saying, "You don't have to keep coming to check in on me. It's not like I'm going anywhere."

"I'm well aware of that."

"Then, why are you here?"

He ran his hand through his hair with a troubled sigh. "Beats the hell out of me."

"Well, since you're here ... Did you say anything to Viper about letting me make a call to work?"

"It's been taken care of."

"What do you mean?"

"I mean ... *it's been taken care of*," he answered sharply.

"Okay ... Then, what about Danny?" I stood up and took a step towards him. "Has he told you what you wanted to know?"

"Why do you keep asking when you know I'm not going to answer?"

"Because I'm hoping if I do, you might actually tell me what the hell is going on."

"That's not going to happen."

"That doesn't mean I'm going to stop asking." Hoping I might be able to get through to him, I took another step closer to him and placed my hand on his arm. "Can you at least tell me if I have any chance—any chance at all—of getting out of here?"

For reasons I didn't understand, I actually believed him when he replied, "If I have anything to say about it, you'll have more than just a chance."

"I really want to believe that."

"Then, believe it." His eyes never left mine as he whispered, "I wouldn't say it if I didn't mean it."

I nodded as I removed my hand from his arm. He was still holding my gaze when a strange expression crossed his face. If I hadn't known better, I would've thought he was thinking about kissing me, especially when his eyes drifted down to my mouth. With each second that passed, the tension between us only grew stronger, suddenly stopping when Hawk grumbled, "Fuck."

Before I had a chance to even think, he turned and disappeared into the hall, locking me inside once again. Out of pure frustration, I threw my hands up in the air and yelled, "What the hell was that?"

Of course, I got no response. Simply more silence. I was done with this insanity. One way or another, I was getting out of this room and as far away from the Sinners' warehouse as I possibly could—even if that meant never seeing him again. I forced that thought out of my head as I collapsed down on the bed and started thinking about my plan to escape. I hadn't been lying there long when the door flew open and Shotgun stepped into the room with a fierce expression on his face. "Time for you to come with me."

"What?" Fearing the worst, I screeched, "Where are you taking me?"

"You'll find out soon enough." He reached for my arm and tugged me out of the room, leading me down the dark hallway. Thinking he might come to my rescue, I looked around for any sign of Hawk, but he was nowhere to be found. My heart raced with panic as the adrenaline started to rush through my veins. I had no idea where he was taking me, but in my gut, I knew it wasn't a place I wanted to go. I tried to pull free from his grasp, but he just held on tighter as he yanked me forward. When we stopped at a door, he looked down at me and barked, "You have five minutes."

He opened the door and shoved me inside. Before I had a chance to figure out what was happening, he shut the door and locked it. I started banging on the door and shouting, "Hey! Let me out!"

"Delilah."

The sound of Danny's voice startled me. I quickly spun around, and the sight of him made my stomach turn. He was sitting in the center of what looked to be some kind of garage with strange tools scattered around the room. Danny's arms were bound behind him, and there was blood all over his clothes. With all the bruising and swelling, his face was almost unrecognizable. I rushed over to him as I cried, "Oh my god, Danny! What have they done to you?"

"I'm all right. Trust me ... it could be a lot worse."

"Who are these guys anyway? Please tell me these aren't your new biker friends."

"No. *Not exactly*."

"Thank God for that." I tried to fight back my tears as I knelt down in front of him. It broke my heart to see my brother like that. "Tell me what can I do."

"Nothing. I got us into this mess, and I'll get us out."

"But how are you—"

"You're just gonna have to trust me, Dee."

"I want to, Danny, but look at you. You're practically hanging by a thread here," I fussed. "And they have me locked in this room and won't tell me anything."

"I know, and I'm sorry about that. I hate that you got pulled into this." An anguished look crossed his face. "You gotta know I never meant for that to happen."

"I do, but that doesn't change the fact that I'm here. Please ... just tell me what's going on."

"I'm sorry, but it's better if you don't know."

"How can it be better? Don't you know I'm going

crazy here?" I argued. "I don't see how it can get any worse, Danny."

"You're wrong. It could be a hell of a lot worse. They could have you in this room, torturing you like they've done me! Don't you get that?"

"Yes, I get it, but they have nothing to gain from doing that to me. I had nothing to do with whatever is going on here."

"Maybe not, but if they think you know something, then—"

"Danny, stop. I know what you're going to say, and I understand why you're concerned, but regardless of what might happen, I deserve to know the truth."

"Damn. You've always been stubborn as hell."

"No more stubborn than you are." I softened my tone as I pleaded, "Just tell me."

With a regretful sigh, he lowered his head in shame. "I got word yesterday that the take I'd delivered to these guys wasn't the real deal. It was counterfeit, and they think I had something to do with it."

"You were dealing drugs?"

He nodded, and just like that, my worst fears had been confirmed. "Dammit, Danny. You know better than to get involved in something like this."

"I don't need a fucking lecture, Delilah."

"I just don't understand why you would do something so stupid. You—"

"I fucked up. I know that. You bitching about it isn't going to make me feel any worse."

"Fine." I sighed. While I didn't like it, I knew he was right. The damage had already been done, so instead of berating him any further, I had to help him find a way out of this mess. "You said the drugs were counterfeit. What does that even mean?"

"It wasn't pure coke. They had probably cut it with something to make it look like the real deal. Hell, I don't even know what they did. The hit I took was legit, just like all the times before, but apparently, the rest of it was trash."

"So, how is any of this your fault if you didn't even know about it?"

"'Cause I'm the one who sold them the goods. Who else are they gonna blame?"

"You really didn't know that the drugs were counterfeit?"

"Hell, no," he answered without hesitation. "I'd have to be all kinds of stupid to try to pull one over on these guys. They don't fuck around."

"Obviously." I lifted my hand to his face, and once again, I had to resist the urge to break out into tears. "What's going to happen to you? To us?"

"I honestly don't know, Delilah. It's bad, really bad, and I had to go and make things even worse by shooting one of them." I could hear the misery in his voice. "I gotta tell ya. I don't think I'll get out of here alive."

"What?"

"It doesn't look good, sis, but there's still hope for you. Just keep your head down, do whatever they tell you to do, and maybe they'll cut you a break."

"No, there has to be something we can do. Some way we can convince them that you were innocent in all this." I stood and started scanning the room. "Maybe there's a way we can get out of here."

"What are you not getting here?" Danny fussed. "You'll

just make things worse if you try to pull something. We have no choice but to ride this out."

"We're supposed to just sit here and wait for them to kill you?" I gasped. "I can't do that, Danny."

Showing little emotion, he replied, "You don't have a choice. They're gonna do what they're gonna do."

"I don't want to lose you."

Before he could respond, the door opened and Hawk stepped inside. Shotgun was standing there next to him, and I knew my conversation with my brother was over. I wanted to resist and stay there with him, but I could tell from their fierce expressions it wasn't a good idea. I stood up and then bent down in front of Danny to lightly kiss him on the forehead and whispered, "I love you. Please don't give up hope."

He didn't respond as he watched me walk over to the men who'd tortured him for hours on end. I couldn't even look at Hawk as I followed them out of the room. I was too angry, too frightened for my brother's life to even speak. We all walked in silence as we made our way down the hall to the room where they'd been keeping me prisoner. I walked in and kept my back to both men as they closed the door and locked me inside. Unable to hold on to my emotions a moment longer, I dropped down on the bed and started to cry. Actually, crying wasn't the word for it. I was a broken, sobbing mess, and no matter how hard I tried, I couldn't stop the tears from falling.

The only thing that kept me from completely losing it was remembering that hairpin in the desk drawer.

HAWK

"Looks like you were right," Shotgun told me as we stood outside Delilah's door. "The girl didn't know shit."

"Doesn't really matter now." It was Shotgun's idea to let Delilah see Danny. He'd hoped that by getting them together that they would talk about everything that had gone down with the take. Just as I feared, that's exactly what happened. "He told her everything."

"Yeah, but at least we can feel certain that we got the truth out of him."

"Let's hope." My chest tightened as I thought back to the expression on Delilah's face when we walked back into the room. I'd expected her to be upset, but she looked completely broken by the sight of her brother. I couldn't blame her. Even though we'd cleaned him up a bit, he still looked like he'd been through hell and back. I glanced over to Shotgun. "What do you think Viper will do about her?"

"Got no idea." He shrugged with indifference. "I would

say it'd depend on whether or not he feels like he can trust her or not. The last thing we need is for her to go running her mouth about any of this. It could cause us some real problems if she did."

He was right. If word got out to the cops that we'd kidnapped her or Danny, much less the fact that we'd done so because of a drug exchange gone bad, we'd be ruined. No way in hell Viper would ever let that happen, nor would I. The club and my brothers meant everything to me. No matter what was going on in my head about Danny's sister, there was no way in hell I'd ever let it come between my brothers and me. I glanced back over to her door and said, "I trust he'll make the right call."

"He always does." He turned and started towards his room. "See you in the morning."

Even after he was long gone, I remained standing outside Delilah's door, listening to the sounds of her muffled cries. Hearing her so upset tore at me, and I had to use every ounce of my restraint not to go into that room and try to console her. Knowing that I would only make matters worse for the both of us, I went to the room across the hall and lay across the bed. I could still hear her crying as I thought about everything we'd learned from Danny's latest interrogation. It wasn't much. In fact, he'd simply confirmed what we already knew. He was just a mule. He, along with several others, would pick up their take from specific locations and distribute it in their territory. Menace was still working on finding out more about Danny's handler in Texarkana, but it hadn't been easy. The guy was smart. He stayed under the radar, used a different burner cell for each one of his associates, and met at different locations for each drop-off. Hell, Menace hadn't even been able to find an official name for the guy. All we had to go on was the name Miller. I was trying to think of a way for us to find out more information on him when I realized I couldn't hear Delilah anymore. Even though I was relieved that she'd finally settled down, I couldn't seem to do the same.

I was lying there trying to clear my head when I heard an odd, scratching sound coming from across the hall. At first, I thought it was just a mouse or one of the guys fucking around, but when it continued for several minutes, I knew it had to be something else. I got out of bed and stepped into the hall. It didn't take me long to realize that the sound was coming from Delilah's room. Being careful not to be heard, I stepped closer to the door, and that's when I realized she was tampering with the lock. Half amazed, half pissed, I stood there glaring at the door, wondering if she had any idea how to pick a fucking lock. I got my answer several minutes later when I heard the lock disengage and the door slowly eased open, revealing a very surprised Delilah. I crossed my arms as I asked, "Going somewhere?"

"What are you doing here?"

"*My job* ... or have you forgotten that I'm supposed to be keeping an eye on you?" I stepped towards her, grabbing her arm as I pulled her back into the room and closed the door behind us. As I took the hairpin from her hand, I asked, "What the hell were you doing? Did you really think you could just walk out of here?"

"I had to at least try," she cried. "Seriously, what else would you expect me to do after I saw what you did to Danny? Just sit here and wait for you to do the same to me?"

"I expected you to do what you were told, Delilah. It's the only way I can help you."

"I don't want your help, Hawk." Her voice trembled with sorrow as she muttered, "How could you do that to Danny? How could you do that to anyone? I just don't get it."

"Some things happen here that are difficult to explain, but there are reasons for everything we do ... including how we've dealt with Danny."

"But he's innocent!" Tears filled her eyes. "He's not the one who tried to trick you, and you know it."

"Maybe not, but he's the only one who can lead us to the person who did," I explained. "And don't forget, he shot one of our brothers."

"And what about me? I didn't have a part to play in any of this."

"I know you didn't."

"But that's not good enough, is it?" She lowered her head as she wiped the tears from her cheek. "I'm never getting out of here, am I?"

"Not like this, you aren't."

"Why does it matter? It doesn't matter what I do. You're still going to kill me, especially now that I know everything and I tried to escape."

"That's never going to happen, Delilah. I'd never hurt you."

"After everything that's happened, how do you expect me to believe that?"

I didn't have the words to explain it to her, so I showed her. I took a step towards her and placed my hand on the nape of her neck, pulling her mouth to mine. The touch of Delilah's lips set me on fire, and I knew right then there was no going back. She felt too good, too right. The scent of her skin and the warmth of her mouth got to me in a way that no woman ever had, and I feared I'd never be able to let her go. My hands made their way past the small of her back down to her perfect ass as I pulled her close against my body. A soft whimper escaped from her lips as they parted, allowing me to kiss her deeper. It was like the world around us faded away and we became lost in each other's arms, but sadly, the moment didn't last long.

Just as my body was becoming hungry for more, Delilah brought her hands up to my chest and gave me a hard push, forcing me to release her. "What the hell are you thinking?"

"Don't try to say you didn't feel something." I crossed my arms as I looked down at her. "'Cause I know you did."

"It doesn't matter if I did. This"—she motioned her hand between us—"can never happen."

"It already has." I turned and headed for the door. Before I walked out, I stopped and said, "You can try and fight it all you want. God knows I have."

She placed her hand on her hip as she sassed, "You're crazy if you think I'd ever want to be with a man like you."

"That kiss just proved otherwise." Before I closed the door, I told her, "Get some sleep, Delilah."

I locked the door and went back across the hall, then collapsed down on the bed. The second I closed my eyes, I found myself thinking back on that fucking kiss—the one that would haunt me until I had her in my arms again. I knew it was fucked up, but I was a selfish asshole and even more stubborn than she was. I wanted to make Delilah mine, and I couldn't just give up and walk away—not without at least trying. I was feeling more determined than ever as I finally drifted off to sleep. As soon as I woke the next morning, I went to check in with Shotgun. When I got down to the room where we were holding Danny, I found him standing in the doorway talking to Viper. As soon as I walked up, Viper announced, "Just the man I wanted to see."

"About?"

"The girl," he answered flatly. "Shotgun was just telling me about her visit with Danny last night. Said it was pretty clear she didn't know anything about him."

"Apparently so."

"Well then, I don't see any point keeping her around. We need to decide what we're going to do with her."

"It's not like we can just let her walk out of here. It's too fucking dangerous." Shotgun ran his hand down his beard as he continued, "If she goes to the cops, we're—"

"Wait, she's just an innocent bystander in all this, and you're saying we should end her?"

"You got another way to handle her? 'Cause Shotgun's right." Viper's eyes narrowed. "If she runs her mouth or even thinks about going to the cops, then—"

"She wouldn't go to them."

"You sound pretty certain of that fact."

"That's because I am. No way in hell she'd do anything to jeopardize Danny's life any more than it already is."

"Not sure that's gonna be enough," Shotgun warned. "She's seen a lot, heard a lot, and we'd be putting everything on the line if we let her walk out of here."

"Then, we make sure she doesn't. We lay it all out. Explain the consequences, and we cover our tracks in case she tries to pull anything." I could tell by Viper's expression that he was surprised by my response. Normally, I'd agree with them both, tell them that the risk was just too fucking high, but I just couldn't do that—not with Delilah. I had two choices. I could either continue my attempt to convince him that she wouldn't rat us out or I could come clean about my unexpected feelings. As I stood there staring back at him, I knew there was only one choice. "We can't kill her, Prez."

"You've gotta be fucking kidding me." Viper knew me better than anyone. He knew my history, knew I'd never spent more than a couple of nights with one chick and liked it that way, so I wasn't surprised when he stepped towards me and asked, "It's only been like a day and a half. You actually gonna tell me you got something for this girl?"

I didn't have to answer. He could tell by the expression on my face. Shaking his head, he chuckled as he replied, "Well, I'll be damned. Never thought I'd see the day."

"I'm just as surprised by the realization as you are, Prez." I exhaled a deep breath as I ran my hand through my hair. "I know it sounds fucking crazy, but there's something about her I just can't shake."

He cocked his eyebrow as he asked, "And how's she going to handle it if she knows your club ends her brother?"

"I'll cross that bridge when we get there."

"And if she does decide to talk?" he pushed.

"Then, I'll handle it."

"I have your word on that?"

I looked him in the eye as I promised, "My loyalty is with you and this club. You gotta know there's nothing I wouldn't do to protect you or my brothers."

"I know that. Just needed to hear you say it." He

thought for a moment, then said, "We've got too much going on for you to be watching over her twenty-four hours a day. Get with Menace. Have him put a tracker on her car ... and monitor all her calls. Once you've sorted that, get with Tripp and Forest. Let them both know they'll be helping you keep an eye on her for the next couple of weeks."

"You got it."

"And bring the girl by my office. I want to have words with her before she's released." As he turned and started down the hall, he stated, "She needs to understand exactly what's at stake before we let her out of here."

"Understood."

Once he was gone, Shotgun looked over to me and asked, "You know I've got your back, but you sure about this, brother?"

"I know it's gotta sound crazy, but yeah. I think it's the right thing to do." I shook my head. "I just hope I don't live to regret it."

"I'll help see to it that you don't."

There was something about his tone that made me wonder exactly what he meant by that declaration, but Shotgun wasn't the kind of man who'd react without reason. Trusting him to do the right thing, I nodded and said, "Thanks, brother."

"Tell Menace I'm here if he needs a hand with anything."

"Will do."

Not wanting to waste any time, I left Shotgun and went to Menace's room to give him the rundown of what we needed to do about Delilah. As I expected, he had no problem getting the tracker set up for her car and was able to route her calls and messages through his systems, enabling him to monitor all calls coming in and out of her phone. Once he had everything covered, I went down to the kitchen to snag some breakfast for Delilah. I grabbed a cup of coffee and a couple of biscuits, then carried them down to her room. When I walked in, she was sitting on the bed looking as beautiful as ever in a pair of black knit leggings and a long sleeve t-shirt. Her damp hair was pulled up in a messy bun, revealing her gorgeous blue eyes that focused solely on the wall in front of her.

She didn't even glance in my direction as I placed her coffee and biscuits on the bedside table. I stepped towards her and stood directly in her line of vision. "We need to talk."

Her eyes drifted away from me and over to the corner of the room as she replied, "There's nothing for us to talk about, Hawk."

"Okay ... Have it your way." I turned and headed towards the door. "I thought you wanted to get out of here. Apparently, I was wrong."

"Wait ... Are you saying I can actually leave?"

"That'll depend on you." I made my way over to her and leaned back against the desk. "I gotta know that you aren't going to do anything stupid."

"Like what?"

"Like run to the cops." My tone grew serious as I explained, "No one can know anything about what's gone down here. *No one*. Danny's life *and yours* will depend on your keeping your mouth shut."

"Okay."

"I'm not fucking around, Delilah. You even think about going to the cops or—"

"I won't say anything. I swear." She stood up to face me as she said, "I'd never do anything to jeopardize Danny's life. My lips are sealed."

"I'm going to hold you to that, and just in case you get any wild ideas, I'll be keeping an eye on you." Her eyes never left mine as I told her, "I'll be monitoring your every move, and—"

"You're going to be stalking me?"

"Call it whatever you want, but I'm not taking any chances. I'm putting a lot on the line by letting you walk out of here."

"What's that supposed to mean?" Her brows furrowed. "Are you saying that you're the reason why I'm getting to leave?"

"That's not important. Just remember what I said. Play this thing smart, and you'll have your life back. One fuck up, and there'll be consequences."

"I won't fuck up."

"Good." As I started towards the door, I told her, "Grab your stuff. It's time to go."

"Wait ... What about Danny? What's going to happen to him?"

"That's not my call."

"How am I supposed to leave here without him?"

"You don't have a choice, Delilah." I got it. She was in a tough spot and I couldn't blame her for being torn, but she had no idea how lucky she was to be given the chance to walk out of here alive. I could've taken the time to explain it to her, but I doubted that it would ease the guilt she was feeling. "You need to remember that Danny got himself into this mess. It'll be up to him to get himself out of it."

Despair crossed her face as she whispered, "But he's my brother, Hawk."

"I get that, I really do, but if Danny's any kind of caring brother at all, he'd want you to get out of here. You gotta know that."

"I know, but—"

"Delilah, get your stuff."

I waited as she quickly grabbed what few belongings she had, then led her down the hall. I expected her to be thrilled about finally getting back to her own life, but she looked even more terrified now than she had when she first arrived, especially when she noticed that we weren't going out to the parking lot. "Where are we going?"

"Viper wants a word with you before you go."

"What?"

When we got to his door, I knocked, then eased it open. "He's waiting inside for you."

"You aren't going in with me?"

"He wanted to talk to you, not me."

"Why do I get the feeling that this isn't going to be a conversation I want to have?"

"He's waiting, Delilah."

She let out a deep breath, then stepped inside his office. I closed the door and waited in the hall for what seemed like an eternity. I had no idea what he was saying to her, but when she came out ten minutes later, I could tell by the horrified expression on her face that he'd made quite an impression on her. I didn't ask her about it. Instead, I led her towards the back door. As we got to the parking lot and walked past a couple of the guys, she wouldn't even look in their direction. Pretending to ignore them, she silently followed me over to my Harley.

When I handed her a helmet, she looked at me like I'd lost my mind. "Wait ... What's this?"

"That is a helmet"—I motioned my hand towards my bike—"and this is a 2019 Road King Classic."

"You don't have a car or something?"

"Nope."

"What about that truck they brought me—"

"Not mine." I threw my leg over the seat and slipped on my helmet. "Unless you wanna stay here, get on."

"But I've ... um ... never ridden a motorcycle before."

"Nothing to it." I took her things out of her hands and placed them in the saddlebags. "You'll see."

When she overheard the guys snickering behind her, she rolled her eyes and put on the helmet. Looking less than pleased, she eased her leg over the seat and settled in behind me. "Okay ... Now what?"

"Just hold on and follow my lead."

Once she'd placed her hands on my hips, I started up the engine and pulled out of the parking lot. The second I pulled onto the main road, Delilah leaned in closer, tightening her grip around my waist, and damn, it felt incredible. That's when it hit me. I'd never had a woman on the back of my bike—at least not one who I'd found remotely memorable. Not a woman like Delilah. I didn't expect to like it as much as I did. I wanted to savor the moment. It was one of the reasons why I chose to take the long way back to Danny's place. When we finally got to his apartment complex, I pulled up next to Delilah's car and parked. As soon as she got off my bike, she asked, "How did you know to come here?"

"I wouldn't be doing my job if I didn't." I reached into my back pocket and pulled out the phone and keys we'd taken from her on the night Shotgun and Rafe brought her to the clubhouse. "You'll need these."

"Thanks."

As she took them from my hand, I told her, "I texted your mother."

"You did?"

"Yeah ... and your boss." She glanced down at the screen, skimming through the messages I'd sent, along with all the missed messages she'd received. "Told them both that you were sick with some stomach thing, so keep that in mind when you talk to them."

"Okay." I grabbed her things out of the saddlebags and handed them to her. She went over and put them in the back seat of her car, then turned back to me. "So, now what?"

"Go home ... Get back to your normal routine, and while you're doing whatever you do, don't breathe a word about the last forty-eight hours."

"What if someone asks me about Danny?"

"You're a smart girl. You'll think of something."

I knew she wasn't happy with my answer—or lack thereof. It was written all over her beautiful face. As fucked up as it might've been, seeing that look on her face made me want her even more. Hell, it took every bit of my restraint to keep my fucking hands off her, especially when I saw the fire in her eyes roar back to life as she stood there glaring at me. After several long, agonizing moments, she started towards her car with all the sass she could muster and spat, "All right then. I guess I'll ... *see you around.*"

"Oh, you'll be seeing me. You can count on that."

DELILAH

"I was worried sick," my mother complained. "I've been trying to call you since you sent that text that you weren't feeling well."

"I know, Mom. I'm sorry I worried you, but I just didn't feel like talking."

"Are you feeling better now?"

"Yes, much better. I think it was just something I ate."

"Well, I'm glad you're feeling better." She paused for a moment, then asked the question I knew was coming. "Did you make it over to Danny's?"

I'd taken a couple of days to collect my thoughts before calling her, hoping I'd be able to come up with something to tell her when she asked me about him. Sadly, nothing had come to mind. I wanted to just tell her the truth. It would've been so much easier—at least it would have been for me. The weight of being the only one who knew was soul crushing, but I simply couldn't tell her what was really going on. Even if I wasn't worried about what Hawk and his friends would do, I knew my mother wouldn't be able to take it. The truth would destroy her. Doing the only thing I could, I lied. "Yes, ma'am. I went by there, but he wasn't home."

"Oh, good heavens. I wonder where that boy could be."

"I don't know, but Mom ... he's old enough to take care of himself. He doesn't need you to worry so much about him."

"But something could've happened to him. He could be in trouble."

Guilt washed over me as I thought back to Danny in that room, beaten and fighting for his life. I quickly swallowed back the emotions that were building in my throat, then said, "He'll be okay, Momma. I'll make sure of it."

"Thank you, sweetie." I heard a commotion in the background, followed by the sound of a man's voice. Before I could ask her what was going on, she said, "I have to go, sweetheart, but I'll call you back tomorrow."

I didn't have a chance to respond before the call ended. My focus was quickly redirected when I heard the rumble of a motorcycle outside. I went over to the window and looked out only to spot Hawk pulling into my parking lot. A cold chill ran down my spine as I noticed him looking in my direction. Cursing under my breath, I quickly stepped out of his line of sight and froze. I'd been driving myself crazy thinking about Danny and what might be happening to him, and knowing Hawk was lurking right outside my apartment was making me even crazier. Partly because I knew if he caught me doing something I shouldn't, he'd kill me, and partly because every time I saw him, I'd start thinking about that kiss—the one that set my entire body on fire, making me feel more alive than I ever had before. The whole thing was insane. I knew that. I just didn't know what the hell I was going to do about it.

The next morning, I decided it was time to get back to work. I'd been gone for four days, and I hoped it would help keep my mind off things. Besides, I missed seeing and talking to the residents there, along with the other nurses I worked with—especially Krissy. She and I had gone to nursing school together and quickly became best friends. We didn't have secrets. We told each other everything ... but not this time. I'd have to use all my restraint to keep what was going on with Danny under wraps—for both our sakes. As soon as I walked through the front doors of the nursing home, Janet stopped me at the front desk with a concerned expression. "What are you doing back? I was expecting you to be out until next week."

"Well... I started feeling better, so I thought I'd come on in and see if you needed me."

"Are you sure?" She cautiously kept her distance as she asked, "Have you been fever free for at least twenty-four hours?"

"I wouldn't be here if I wasn't." Janet was a stickler for the rules, so I wasn't at all surprised by her question. She would never want to put any of our patients in danger, and I hoped she knew I felt the same way. I smiled as I reassured her, "I'm fine, Janet. I don't even think it was really the stomach bug. I think it was just bad sushi or something else I ate."

"Well, that's good to hear because we could really use the help today. Carol and Nikki both called in with the flu, and Mr. McClanahan and Ms. Rice have been all out of sorts. I can't seem to get either of them settled."

"I'll see what I can do." I put my purse and keys in the desk drawer, then asked, "Is Ms. Rice in her room?"

"Yes, but be forewarned, she's not herself today."

"Thanks for the heads up."

I started down the hall, and when I walked into Ms. Rice's room, I could see what Janet was talking about. Ms. Rice was normally very social, spending most of her days visiting with her friends or watching her favorite game shows, but today, she was sitting in the corner of her room alone. She was still in her robe, and instead of watching TV, she was staring out the window with the saddest expression I'd ever seen. My heart ached for her as I walked over and knelt down beside her. I placed my hand on her arm as I smiled and said, "Hey there, Ms. Rice. How you making it today?"

She didn't even acknowledge my presence—not so much as a blink. I didn't know what to think. Ms. Rice was younger than most of the residents, so her mind was still pretty sharp. Her health was a different matter. She had moved into our facility after she fell and fractured her hip, and because of one complication after the next, she'd been with us for over two years. Thankfully, that hadn't broken her spirit. She'd always smile and look tickled to see me whenever I came to her room to do my rounds. We'd talk about her day and whether or not she'd spoken to her daughter, but today she seemed like she was a million miles away. Hoping I might be able to get to her, I just started talking like we normally did. "I'm sorry I haven't been to see you in a couple of days. I was sick with this stomach bug thing, but I'm feeling a lot better now. How have you been feeling? Aren't you going to watch your shows this morning?"

I waited for a moment, hoping she might say something. She didn't. I wasn't ready to give up, so I said, "Well, if not, I'm sure you can get caught up with them later. Has Leslie called or come by?"

At the sound of her daughter's name, Ms. Rice turned and looked at me, letting me know I'd struck a chord. After several moments, she finally muttered, "Leslie's sick. She has the flu and won't be able to come see me."

"Is that what has you so upset?"

"I'm just so worried about her and the children. Things have been so hard for her since Tim left her. I just wish I could do more for them."

"I understand why you might be worried, but Leslie will bounce back from this. The kids have gotten older, too, so they can help look after their mom." I gave her leg a little pat as I assured her, "You'll see. Leslie will be back on her feet in no time."

"I'm sure you're right, but I still worry."

"Of course, you do. You're her mother. It's your job to worry about her, but everything's going to be okay." I could tell she wasn't completely convinced, so I asked, "What if I gave Leslie a call this morning? I could check on her and see how she's feeling for you. Would that make you feel better?"

"Oh, yes. That would be wonderful."

"Then consider it done." As I stood up, I asked, "Can I do anything for you before I go? Walk you down to the cafeteria for some breakfast or turn on one of your shows?"

"I'm fine for now." She smiled. "I'll turn it on in a minute."

"Okay. I'll let you know when I get in touch with Leslie."

"Thank you, dear."

"No problem." As I started towards the door, I told her, "Just give me a shout if you need me."

I left her room with every intention of going to find Mr. McClanahan, but as I walked down the hall, I was sidetracked by Krissy. She came running up to me with a big smile on her face. "Thank god, you're back! I don't know if I could take another day in this place without you."

"Been that bad, huh?"

"It's been insane, but no more than usual. I just didn't realize how much better things are when you're around." She leaned towards me and whispered, "Janet has been a mega-twat the last few days. Word is, she's been all pissy because she got a bad eval from—"

Before she could finish her sentence, Lacey, another one of the nurses, called out to her and said, "Hey, Krissy! Can you give me a hand with Mr. Larkin? I need to change his bedding."

"Sure thing," she answered before turning her attention back to me. "I'll catch you up at lunch break."

"Sounds good."

As soon as Krissy left to go help Lacey, I tried once again to make my way down to Mr. McClanahan's room. Unlike Ms. Rice, he was older, and while his health was better than Ms. Rice's, his mind was not. He preferred to be alone, often isolating himself in his room for days, and the rare times he was around others, he was often antagonistic, starting arguments over petty things. Mr. McClanahan was easily set off, so Janet ordered all the nurses to limit their interactions with him and only do mandatory routine checks. Considering his normal temperament, hearing that he was in rare form today was more than a little concerning. As I quietly slipped into his room, I was expecting to find him angry, hostile, and ready to start an argument, but that's not what I found at all.

Mr. McClanahan was sitting in his chair and actually smiling. I was shocked to find Hawk sitting there with him. When I realized they were in the midst of a deep conversation, I took a step back and listened. Hawk smiled as he asked, "What'd ya ride?"

"Last bike I had was a Yamaha TX50." Mr. McClanahan chuckled as he said, "I know you boys today are all about your Harleys, but let me tell ya, that Yamaha was one hell of a ride."

"I bet it was. Nothing better than being out on the road, no matter what you're riding."

"You're right about that."

"So, how long has it been?"

"Too damn long ... at least twenty years, maybe more." Mr. McClanahan sighed as he continued, "Some of the best days of my life were spent with my brothers. Would give anything to go back, but I'm grateful God graced me with memories."

I couldn't believe it. Mr. McClanahan looked happier than I'd ever seen him. Hell, the man was practically beaming, and it was all because of Hawk. I didn't know what to think. I had no idea what he was even doing there. It was one thing to watch me from a distance, but Hawk had taken things to a new level when he actually came inside. I should've been furious, but as I stood there watching him with Mr. McClanahan, I was far from angry. Instead, I was in awe. Hawk was not only able to get our grumpiest resident to carry on a lengthy conversation, but he'd gotten him to smile—even chuckle a time or two. It was impossible not to be moved by the sight. I wiped a tear from the corner of my eye as I listened to Hawk say, "Maybe we can find a way to get you back on the road again."

"Doubt that's ever gonna happen, son. I'm just not as able as I used to be."

"I don't know. I think you've still got at least one more good ride in ya."

While it was thoughtful of Hawk to even think about getting Mr. McClanahan out for a ride, I didn't want him to make a promise he couldn't possibly keep, so I stepped out of hiding and said, "Hi there, Mr. McClanahan. I see you have company today."

"I sure do," he replied proudly. "Not sure if you've met, but this is Hawk."

I cocked my eyebrow at Hawk as I replied, "Yes. We've crossed paths before."

"That we have." Hawk stood up and extended his hand to Mr. McClanahan then said, "It was good talking to you, brother. Mind if I stop by again sometime?"

Mr. McClanahan shook his hand. "No, not at all. I'd like that."

"Good. I'll see you soon."

Without saying a word to me, Hawk walked past me and into the hall. Before I even realized what I was doing, I rushed out the door. "Hawk!"

He stopped and turned to look at me, and the second his eyes met mine, a shiver ran down my spine, making me instantly regret chasing after him. I couldn't understand it, but there was something about the man that I found hard to resist. The fact that he looked unbelievably sexy in his tattered jeans, dark t-shirt, and leather vest didn't help matters. His green eyes danced with mischief as he said, "Yeah?"

"What are you doing here?"

"I think it's pretty clear. I was talking to Mr. McClanahan."

"You know what I mean." I let out a huff. "Why are you here ... inside where I work? I mean, it's one thing to follow me and watch me like you've been doing, but this is too much."

"Just so we're clear, I wasn't planning on coming inside."

"Then, why did you?"

"'Cause I had to take piss," he answered bluntly.

"Oh."

"I've got things to do, so ... unless you have something else on your mind, I've gotta get going."

"No, I didn't need anything else."

I watched as he turned and headed towards the front doors of the building. Just before he walked outside, he called, "I'll be seeing ya, Delilah."

I was too frustrated to respond. I could only stand there watching as he strolled out and into the parking lot. I was still standing there trying to wrap my head around what had just taken place when Krissy came rushing up to me. "Was it just my imagination, or did I just see you talking to maybe the hottest guy I've ever laid my eyes on?"

"It was your imagination."

"Come on, Delilah," she fussed. "Who was that?"

"That was nobody, or at least, nobody you'd want to know. *Trust me.*"

Before she could ask anything more, I turned and went to check on Mr. McClanahan. As soon as I was certain he was okay, I went back to the nurses' desk to find Ms. Rice's file. Once I found her daughter's phone number, I gave her a quick call to make sure she was okay. She assured me that she was fine, and thanked me for looking after her mother. By the time I shared the news with Ms. Rice, it was time to get lunch to all the residents who couldn't make it to the cafeteria. My busy morning turned into an even busier afternoon, which was just fine. I liked having the distraction as it kept my mind off things. I was thankful that work continued to stay that way over the next few days. I was actually starting to feel like my life was getting back to normal—at least, as normal as it could be under the circumstances. Sadly, the feeling was short-lived.

After another long day at work, I ran a few errands, then headed back to my apartment. I'd just gotten out of my car, my hands full of groceries, and I was on my way up to the front door. That's when a strange shadow in one of the trees caught my attention. I stepped closer, trying to get a better look through the thick leaves, and was surprised to find Hawk perched on one of the larger branches.

"Seriously?" He looked down at me with surprise. "You're hiding out in trees now?"

"What?"

"You heard me. It's bad enough that you stalked me at work, but now—"

"Delilah," he warned as he motioned his head to the left.

When I turned to look, I found my elderly neighbor, Mrs. Tate, standing beneath the tree. "Mrs. Tate ... I, um ... I didn't see you standing there."

"I've been trying to get Mr. Twiddles down from that tree for over an hour when this sweet boy came over and offered to help." She tightened her grip on the lapel of her tattered pink bathrobe. "Isn't he just the nicest young man?"

"Um-hmm." I couldn't believe my eyes. Mr. Rough and Tough was actually attempting to rescue my neighbor's cat. Mrs. Tate looked up at Hawk like he was some kind of superhero as he continued further up the tree. When he got close enough, he reached out and grabbed the overweight orange tabby, carefully cradling him in his arms before starting back down. As soon as he got close enough, I asked, "You need a hand?"

Hawk shook his head as he made his way to the ground. "No, I've got it."

"Thank you so much," Mrs. Tate cried as she reached for Mr. Twiddles, kissing him as she cuddled him close to her chest. "You bad boy. You had me worried sick. I thought I'd lost you."

"He's all safe and sound now."

"Thanks to you," she replied. "I can't thank you enough."

"Don't mention it. I was glad to help."

Mrs. Tate looked down at her cat as she said, "I better get him inside. Thank you again."

Hawk and I watched in silence as she shuffled up the steps and into her apartment. Once she'd made it inside,

Hawk turned his attention to me. "Well, I guess I best get going... unless you need a hand with those groceries."

"I'm good." I wasn't sure how to take Hawk actually being sweet. It made it harder to remember that he was one of the men who'd bought drugs from my brother and later tortured him. I wanted to believe that I'd witnessed another side to him—a side that was good, compassionate, and worth getting to know. It wasn't that hard to believe. After all, he'd saved the day with both Mr. McClanahan and Mrs. Tate, so there was a possibility that there was more to him than I realized. The push and pull of it all was driving me nuts. I couldn't take it anymore. I had to know for sure. It was the only way I'd ever be able to get him out of my head. Before I had a chance to talk myself out of it, I glanced down at my groceries and said, "I was planning on making dinner. Since you're here and all, would you like to join me?"

HAWK

I'd had a hell of a day. Actually, I'd had a hell of a week. After going over everything we'd learned from Danny, we decided it was time for us to set up a meet with his handler. We'd have Danny call him with another large order, and when he went to meet up with Miller to pick it up, we'd be there. One way or another, we would get the answers we were looking for. While we were dealing with the Danny bullshit, we were also busy trying to get the new strip club up and running. Viper had gotten the permits we needed, and we'd started up construction. Some of the bigger stuff, like electrical and plumbing, had been hired out, but the brothers and I were doing what we could to take care of the rest. Viper wanted the business running as quickly as possible, so we'd been at it night and day, busting our asses to get it all done. By the time we finished installing the drywall in the main bar, I was exhausted and in need of a break. I went to the clubhouse and took a hot shower with the intention of calling it an early night, but as soon as I got out, I decided to get dressed and head off on my bike. The next thing I knew, I was parked outside of Delilah's apartment.

I'd checked the tracker on her car. I knew she hadn't made it home yet, but there I sat, waiting for her red two-door sedan to pull up. I told myself that I just needed a quick glimpse of her to make sure that she was okay, and then I'd go. It seemed like a simple plan until Mrs. Tate came along. Poor thing stood out there for over twenty minutes calling that damn cat, but he refused to come down. I felt sorry for the lady, so I went over and offered to help. I never imagined that Delilah would walk up just as I got up in that damn tree. I managed to get the cat down, and for my efforts, I got an invitation to dinner. I hadn't intended on staying, but there was no way in hell I was going to pass up a chance to be alone with Delilah. I tried not to sound too eager when I replied, "Yeah, I'd like that."

"Great." She smiled as she started towards the door. "Come on up."

I followed her inside and up a flight of stairs, and a minute later, we were walking into her apartment. It was small, just one-bedroom with a little kitchen and living room, but it was full of southern charm and sass—just like Delilah. As I followed her over to the kitchen, I told her, "Nice place."

"Thanks." She placed the bags of groceries on the counter, then started putting them away. "It's not much, but it's close to work and I like my neighbors."

"How long have you lived here?"

"About four months ... maybe a little longer." She placed a thick salmon filet on a pan and started to season it. "Baked salmon okay?"

"Yeah, that'd be great. Can I give you a hand with something?"

"You could peel these." She handed me the bag of potatoes as she pointed over to the stove. "There's a peeler thingie in the drawer next to the stove."

"Got it."

After I grabbed it out of the drawer, I went over to the sink and got to work. My back was to her when she asked, "Can I get you a soda or a beer?"

"A beer would be good." I heard the refrigerator door open, and seconds later she placed the bottle on the counter next to me. "Thanks."

"No problem." I could feel her eyes on me as she stood there for a moment, silently watching me before walking back over to the stove. As she started seasoning the salmon, she asked, "Can I ask you a question?"

"What's on your mind?"

"I was just thinking about your real name. I'm guessing it isn't Hawk."

"No, it isn't." I chuckled. "That's my road name. My real name is Zander Michaels."

"Zander. Hmm ... I was thinking it would be something more like Malachi or Isaac." she teased.

"*Malachi*, huh?"

"Yeah," she giggled, "*he who walks behind the rows* ... and all that."

"You're a smartass. That's all there is to it."

"Just calling 'em like I see 'em, *Zander*." I won't deny that there was a slight awkwardness between us. Hell, I'd be a fool to think that things would just be easy with all that had gone down with her brother, but moments like this made me wonder if we could find our way around it all. She turned her attention back to the salmon, and once she had it all prepped, she slipped it into the oven. When I finished the potatoes, she sliced them up and placed them in a pot. Her back was to me as she said, "You know, you've never really told me anything about the Ruthless Sinners. I'm guessing from all the motorcycles and leather, you're a motorcycle gang or something."

"Not a gang. We're an MC." She glanced back at me with a confused look on her face, so I explained, "It's pretty simple. A gang is about finding the means to an end, while an MC is all about the brotherhood. We're family. Simple as that."

"And you all live in that warehouse building together?"

"The clubhouse?" She nodded. "No. We don't all live there, but we have rooms there so we can stay whenever need be."

"So, you have a place of your own?"

"Yeah. I have a house not too far from here."

"A house? Hmm ... That must be nice. I couldn't even begin to afford a place of my own ... at least not yet. Maybe someday, though." After checking the stove one last time, she turned to me and said, "It's going to be a few minutes before it's ready. I'm going to run and take a shower. I have to get out of these scrubs."

"Okay. Take your time."

"Make yourself at home." She started towards her room and said, "Oh, and umm ... make sure the potatoes don't burn."

"I've got it covered."

Seconds later, I heard the water turn on, so I took a moment to look around her place. Wasn't much to see, just a few pictures scattered here and there, but the photographs of her friends and family gave me a little insight into her life. There was no picture of a dad or grandparents, only a few her mother and Danny, and a couple of others of Delilah and a cute blonde. I'd just gone into the kitchen and finished checking the potatoes when Delilah returned. The sight of her nearly took my breath away. The crazy thing about it was that she wasn't even fixed up. Her long hair was down and she was wearing a pair of baggy sweats with a black tank top, but she looked fucking incredible. A smile crept across her face as she asked, "You ready to eat?"

"Always."

I helped her bring everything over to the small kitchen table, then we sat down and made our plates. As we started eating, our previous small talk fired up once again. We both shared a couple of stories about our childhood, and Delilah told me about her parents' divorce and how they'd all moved into her grandmother's house. From what I'd heard, divorce was tough on most kids, but I got the impression it wasn't so bad for Delilah. In fact, from the way she talked, her mother walking out on their father was the best thing that could've happened to them. Our conversation continued as we cleaned up the dirty dishes and made our way over to the sofa. Delilah reached for the remote, and a smile crossed her face when she saw that *Animal Kingdom* was on. She looked over to me and said, "I can't believe you actually watch this."

"Are you kidding? It's one of my favorites."

"Seriously?"

"Definitely." I chuckled. "Those brothers pull off some pretty impressive shit, and you were right about Smurf. She's crazy, but damn, they'd never make it without her."

"I think Jay is up to something."

"Yeah, I think so, too. I just don't have any idea what."

We both sat back and watched the show, occasionally discussing different aspects of it. As soon as it was over, she turned off the TV, and we went right back to talking. We sat inches apart, telling one story after the next. I'd just finished going on about the day my father had bought me my first motorcycle when it hit me. I wasn't a man who did "small talk." I sure as hell wasn't one to talk about myself, but she drew it out of me, making me want to share things with her I'd never told anyone. The realization got to me, but not enough to make me get up and leave. Instead, I sat there and surprisingly relished every moment I got to spend with her.

The sun had set, and it was starting to get late when a fretful expression crossed Delilah's face. I thought she was going to send me walking, but instead, she asked, "I know I'm not supposed to ask, but is Danny okay?"

The club's dealing with Danny wasn't something I could discuss with her. Club business was always kept solely between the brothers, but I decided it wouldn't hurt to tell her, "He's hanging in there."

"Do you think there's a chance he'll walk away from this?"

That wasn't a question I was ready to answer. Unfortunately, I knew this was something she wouldn't let it go. "The decision isn't up to me, but there's always a chance."

"But he wasn't the one responsible for the mix-up."

"He knew there was a problem, and instead of coming to us about it, he tried to skip town. And on top of that, he shot one of my brothers, Delilah. He could've killed Rafe."

The vulnerable look in her eyes masked a strength

inside of her that even she didn't know existed, but I knew it was there. It was evident when she disputed again, *"But he didn't kill him."*

"No, but he knew there would be consequences to his actions when he pulled the trigger. That's on him." Anguish crossed her face, and it gutted me to see her so worried. Hoping to ease her mind, I explained, "Viper is our president for a reason. He doesn't make rash decisions. He thinks things through and does what's right for everyone concerned. I trust he'll do the same when it comes to Danny."

"You know ... I shouldn't even be sitting here with you right now. You kidnapped me and locked me away in that room. I saw what y'all did to my brother. And after all that, I should hate the very sight of you, but for some reason ... *I don't*. I actually like being with you"—she looked at me, her eyes full of doubt—"much more than I should. How crazy is that?"

"I don't think you're crazy at all. Actually, I think you're probably one of the sanest people I know."

"I'm not sure that's a good thing." She teased with a giggle.

"Trust me. It's a good thing ... a very good thing."

She sat there, silently staring at me, and I knew then it was time for me to make a choice. I could take a chance with her or walk away before things got even more complicated. The decision might've been easier if she didn't look so damn beautiful looking at me with those gorgeous blue eyes, waiting for me to make my move. So, I took a chance. I reached for Delilah and pulled her over to me, then pressed my mouth against hers. Drawing her in closer she didn't resist, instead she kissed me back.

Need surged through me like a fucking wildfire. I feared if I didn't extinguish the burn, it would completely consume me. I knew she felt the same just by the way she whispered my name. "Zander."

I stood up and turned to face the couch, then leaned forward to pick her up. My hands cupped under her perfect ass, and as I lifted her, she slipped her arms around my neck while her legs instinctively wrapped around my waist. My breath caught when I felt her body pressed against mine. Damn. As I started towards her room, I had to fight the urge to stop and just take her right there on the fucking floor. When we finally made it to her room, I carried her to the foot of the bed and slowly lowered her feet to the floor. With her standing before me, I brought my hand up to her face, and ran the pad of my thumb across her bottom lip. Her eyes flashed with desire as she whispered, "This is a probably bad idea."

"Maybe, but it sure as hell feels right."

"So, maybe I'm not that crazy after all."

My eyes never left hers as she slipped her arms around my neck. She studied me for a moment, then drew me closer, pressing her mouth against mine. When we kissed earlier, it was soft and slow. This kiss was different. This was filled with a hunger that matched my own, and I simply couldn't resist the temptation. Delilah's body melted into me as her tongue brushed again mine—and then it was over. I'd had all I could take. I had wanted Delilah since the moment I laid eyes on her, and I was damn well going to have her. I pushed up the hem of her tank top, the tips of my fingers skimming over her soft skin as I lifted it over her head.

A soft whimper escaped her lips when I pulled her body closer to mine. My hand reached for the nape of her neck as I eased back and asked, "You sure about this?"

She nodded, then said, "I didn't know it was possible to want someone like I want you right now."

Her hands reached behind her back as she unhooked and removed her black lace bra, exposing her perfect, firm breasts. Damn. She didn't shy away from me as I watched her loosen the string to her sweatpants and slowly inch them down her long, slender legs. She just stood there in a pair of black panties with her long red hair flowing down around her delicate shoulders. "So fucking beautiful."

I quickly lifted my t-shirt over my head, tossing it to the side. I could hardly restrain myself with her standing there, watching with anticipation as I started to remove the rest of my clothes. I pulled off my boots and socks, and when I lowered my jeans and boxers down my hips, the tip of her tongue slowly dragged across her bottom lip.

Delilah stood there staring at me with needful eyes as I took my aching cock in my hand and gave it a hard squeeze, trying to relieve some of the throbbing pressure that had been building since the moment we'd first kissed. I could feel my pulse raging against my fingers as I slowly stroked it, groaning out a curse as I felt it continue to harden in my grip. Delilah stepped closer, her eyes totally focused on the motion of my hand before replacing it with her own as she took hold of my cock.

Her caresses were long and firm as she stroked back and forth along my hard, thick shaft, making it damn near impossible not to come right then and there. I wouldn't let that happen though. When I couldn't take it a any longer, I tossed her sexy little body onto the bed. Anticipation flashed through her eyes as her hands dropped to her hips. She quickly lowered her panties, inch by inch, down her long, sexy legs, taunting me. Once she'd kicked them off of the bed, she inched back, her gorgeous, naked body sprawled across the sheets. As I looked down at her, I couldn't imagine a more stunning sight. Every fiber of my being ached for her. "You got any idea how fucking beautiful you are?"

I didn't wait for her to answer. I needed to taste her, to see for myself just how turned on she really was. I lowered myself down on the bed and settled between her thighs, then spread them wide as I raked my tongue firmly across her clit. Her fingers wound into the sheets, twisting them in her hands, as I continued to tease her with my mouth. I never took my eyes off of hers as I relentlessly licked and sucked, back and forth, relishing the way her body reacted to my every touch.

The warmth of her naked body enveloped me, and I could feel my need for her building, burning deep inside my gut. *Fuck*. My hands slid under her ass, pulling her closer to my mouth. Then, her fingers dug into my hair and she arched her back off the bed as I pressed the flat of my tongue against her sensitive flesh. She was close to the edge, and I couldn't wait a minute longer. I had to be inside her, so I reached for my jeans and grabbed a condom out of my wallet. I rolled it on and hovered over her as I raked my throbbing cock against her clit.

"I'm going to fuck you now, Delilah, and when I'm done, I'm going to fuck you again. The question is, which way do you want it first ... *slow and deep* or *rough and fast?*"

Her eyes never left mine as she whispered, "Rough and fast."

As soon as the words left her mouth, I slammed deep inside. A rush of air hissed through her teeth as I withdrew and drove into her again and again. I'd imagined the moment many times over the past few days, each time more detailed than the last, but never had I dreamed it would feel so fucking good.

"Fuck, your pussy is so fucking tight." I growled and started thrusting harder and deeper with every drive, building up to a relentless pace. I wanted to see her orgasm take hold, to watch her body grow rigid as she found her release and screamed out my name. Her head reared back and her moans filled the room. That was it. That was exactly what I fucking wanted to hear. She dug her nails into my lower back as her hips bucked against mine, meeting my every thrust with more force and more intensity. I could feel the pressure building, causing a growl from my chest.

"Fuck," I groaned as she tightened around me. She panted wildly, and her thighs clamped down around my hips when I tried to increase my pace. I knew she was close, unable to stop the inevitable torment of her building release. I lowered my hand in between us and raked my thumb across her clit, and that's all it took. The muscles in her body grew taut as her orgasm took hold. I continued to drive into her, the sounds of my body pounding against hers and echoing throughout the room until I finally came inside her. With a ragged breath, I lay down beside her, after quickly tossing the condom in the trash next to the bed. I rolled to my side, pulling her over to me, and the room stilled as she nestled up next to me.

We both lay there, staring up at the ceiling in a haze, and I'd barely had a chance to catch my breath when Delilah looked up at me with a mischievous smile. "You got something on your mind?"

"I was just wondering when I'm gonna get it 'slow and hard.'"

DELILAH

My night with Zander was incredible. My morning with him was more of the same, but as soon as he walked out the door, a wave of guilt washed over me. My brother was fighting for his life, and I'd just had sex with one of the men who held his future in his hand. To make matters worse, it was the best sex I'd ever had. When I was with him, I'd never felt so alive, so consumed by a man's touch, and my body was already aching for more. Hoping I might come to my senses, I got up and took a long hot shower. Unfortunately, I was still thinking about him even after I got dressed and was on my way to my car. I even found myself looking for him as I turned into the parking lot of my work, but there was no sign of him or his brothers. The same held true the following two days. There were no calls, no casual check-ins, or so much as a drive-by since we'd slept together, and I silently cursed myself for being disappointed by the fact.

I guess I shouldn't have been surprised. It wasn't like

anything could've come from our night together. We were from two different worlds, and there was just too much for us to overcome. Sadly, the thought didn't ease the tightness in my chest as I got ready for another day of work. I grabbed my things and headed to nursing home; once I got there, I wasted no time making my rounds, checking in on my assigned residents and making sure they had everything they needed. I was pleased to see that both Mrs. Rice and Mr. McClanahan were both in good spirits. It seemed that Zander's visit with Mr. McClanahan had made a lasting impression. As I thought about it, I realized Zander had made a lasting impression on me as well. No matter how hard I tried, I couldn't stop thinking about him or why I hadn't seen or heard from him, so much so that Krissy called me out on it. She walked up to me with a look of pure determination, placed her hand on her hip, and snapped, "What's up with you?"

"Nothing is up with me. I'm ... uh, fine."

"Um-hmm." She crossed her arms as she stood there studying me. "The other day you came in here practically glowing, and now you look like someone kicked your dog."

"I never had a glow, Krissy."

"Oh, yeah. You most definitely did," she argued. "I kept thinking you were going to tell me about the guy, but nope, you've just been walking around here keeping your little secret all to yourself."

"What makes you think there's a guy?"

"Because I know you, and it's written all over your face. Your cheeks were all flushed and you had a little sparkle in your eye. So, who was it? Cameron?" Without giving me a chance to respond, she shook her head. "No, you sent that douchebag packing months ago, so it had to be a new guy ... Oh! Was it that fine ass who came by here the other day—the one who won over Mr. McClanahan? *Oh, my jeez.* Please tell me it was him! He was some kind of hot. I would've climbed that man like a tree."

Reading my expression, her mouth dropped open and her eyes widened. "Oh, my god. It was him!! You banged the hot guy from the other day!"

"I have no idea who or what you're talking about."

"Oh please." She shook her head. "I don't know why you're trying to keep it a secret. You know you've never been able to lie to me."

"I know. It's not that I'm trying to lie about it. It's just ... It's umm ... complicated."

"Why is it complicated?"

"Because he isn't a good guy."

"All the better," she snickered. "Bad boys are *always* good in bed."

"Krissy, it's not that simple."

"It could be if you'd just let it." Krissy crossed her arms and smirked. "Just have a little fun with the guy and leave all the complicated crap out of it."

"I don't know if that's possible, Krissy. *Not with this guy.* Besides, I haven't seen or heard from him since that night."

"Maybe he's been busy or ... he doesn't want to come off too eager."

"Um-hmm." I rolled my eyes. "I doubt that's the case."

A warm smile crossed her face as she said, "I tell you what ... let's go out tonight. We'll have a few drinks, dance a little, and we'll figure this thing out together."

I always had a great time whenever I went out with Krissy, but I'd never been able to keep secrets from her, especially when I was drinking. I was scared I might say something I shouldn't. "I don't know. I'm really tired and—"

"No excuses." She cut me off. "We're going."

"Ugh ... okay, fine."

"Great. I'll be over at your place around eight to pick you up, and wear something cute—maybe one of those little dresses you never want to wear."

"You mean the ones that make me look like a hooker with my ass hanging out?"

"Yep." As she started to walk away, she argued, "You don't look like a hooker. You look amazing, and you know it."

She disappeared into one of the resident's room, and I didn't see her again until our shift was over. As we made our way out to the parking lot, Krissy reminded me that she'd be at my place at eight, and before I had a chance to back out, she hopped in her car and started the engine. After she pulled out of the parking lot, I took a quick look around and checked to see if there was any sign of Zander. When there wasn't, I grumbled under my breath and dragged myself to my car, then drove back to my apartment to get ready. Even though I was in no mood to go out barhopping, I took a shower, fixed my hair and makeup, and put on one of those little dresses like Krissy had requested. I'd just finished getting ready when she knocked on the door. As soon as I answered, her eyes widened with approval as she said, "Ooh, la la, *mamasita*. You are looking fine tonight."

"I take it you approve?"

"Girl, you know I do. Give me a twirl." I turned around in a circle, showing off the fitted red dress I'd only worn once before. It wasn't something I would typically wear since it was so short, but Krissy clearly approved. "You look amazing."

"Thank you. You look great too." Krissy never failed to look incredible whenever we went out. Tonight was no different. Her blonde hair was pulled back, and she wore a black miniskirt with a sparkly halter top that showed off just the right amount of cleavage. "The guys are gonna be all over you in that."

A mischievous smirk crossed her face as she said, "I certainly hope so."

Once I grabbed my things, I followed her downstairs and out to the cab she had waiting for us. Once again, I saw no sign of Zander as we pulled out of the parking lot and headed downtown. We had the cab drop us off at a corner near one of our favorite little diners. After we were seated, we ordered a quick bite, chatted about work while we ate, then walked down to Music Row. There were several great bars along the strip, and as always, each one of them was packed. As we started making our way through the crowd, Krissy took my hand, and in a matter of minutes, we were sitting at the bar of one of the more popular places in town.

When the bartender came over, Krissy ordered us each two double shots of tequila.

"What the hell, Krissy!" I fussed. "I have to work tomorrow."

"Oh, come on. When's the last time you had a couple of drinks," she argued as she handed me one of the tall shot glasses. "Live a little."

"Okay, but no complaining when my ass is dragging tomorrow."

"I won't say a word," she lied.

She tilted her head back, downing the double shot with one big chug, then watched as I did the same. Once we'd done it again with the second, she ordered us a couple of mixed drinks. After a little searching, we found a table in the back and quickly claimed it as our own. The alcohol was just starting to take effect when Krissy leaned towards me and said, "Tell me all about him."

"Honestly, I don't know much about him."

"Well, you had to know something ... you slept with the guy."

"Yeah, but I think we just got caught up in the moment or something."

"That wouldn't be hard to do, especially with a guy as hot as him." She giggled as she questioned, "Where did you meet him anyway?"

I'd never been able to lie to her, so I tried bending the truth instead. "We crossed paths the night I went to check on Danny. I kind of thought he was an asshole at the time, but that day he came to work and talked to Mr. McClanahan ... I saw a different side to him, a side I really liked, but like I said, I haven't heard from him since we slept together."

"So, he's a player, huh?"

"I don't know, but so far, he hasn't proven otherwise."

"Well, two can play that game." Krissy slid my drink over to me and said, "There are plenty of hot guys here tonight. It's time to party."

"I think that's a great idea."

We both finished off our drinks, then headed out to

the dance floor. It was the first time since the night we were together that I wasn't thinking about Zander or why I hadn't seen or heard from him. Instead, I danced with my friend and let go of all those thoughts that'd been weighing on me. The two of us had broken out in a sweat, so we went back to our table and ordered another round of drinks. We were just about to finish them off when I reached into my purse for my phone. I had no idea what had possessed me to check my messages, but I got quite a surprise when I noticed a text from a number I didn't recognize.

Unknown Number:
What are you doing?

As soon as I read it, I knew it was from him. I don't know how, but I just did. I also knew it wasn't merely a simple message from a friend asking what I was up to. No. This message was entirely different, a warning of sorts, but I didn't care. I wasn't going to play into Zander's hand. He didn't have the right to question me in such a way, not after blowing me off. I considered responding with a chastising message, telling him to go to hell, but decided that ignoring him would be much more effective. Feeling confident in my decision, I put my phone back in my purse, finished my drink, then turned to Krissy. "Are you ready to get back out there?"

"Girl, you know it."

She smiled and then followed me out onto the dance floor. We hadn't been there long, when two guys came up and started dancing alongside us. Soon after Krissy started flirting with one of them, and they quickly got carried away. His friend kept a courteous distance, but it was clear from his intense stare that he was interested. He was good-looking, tall with blond hair and hazel eyes, and physically fit, but sadly, when I looked at him, my heart didn't race the way it had with Zander. In fact, my heart wasn't in it at all, even when the music turned slow and he took me in his arms and we swayed to the rhythm. I should've just danced along and pretended that I wasn't bothered by the fact he wasn't Zander, but I simply couldn't do it. Disappointment crossed his face as I stepped back and said, "Thanks for the dance, but I've really got to go."

"Oh … okay." He gave me a slight smile and said, "Maybe we can do it again sometime."

"Yeah … maybe."

I hadn't gotten far when Krissy called out to me, "Hey, Dee! Where ya going?"

I turned to face her as I answered, "I'm gonna go. I'm just not feeling it tonight."

"What? We're just starting to have fun." She motioned her hand back towards the dance floor. "Those guys are totally into us."

"I know, but I'm just—"

Before I could finish my answer, a surprised look crossed her face as she muttered, "Oh, my god."

"What?"

"Umm … *He's here.*"

"Who's here?"

I quickly turned to see who she was talking about, and that's when I noticed Zander walking in our direction.

His eyes were trained on me as he plowed through the crowd with an intense expression marking his handsome face. When he made his way over to us, he reached for my hand and started walking towards the front door. I jerked my hand away from his. "What the hell do you think you're doing?"

"I'm taking you home."

"I'm not ready to go home, and I'm certainly not going home with you." My drinks had clearly caught up with me when I slurred, "So, you can just put that in your pipe and smoke it."

"You've been drinking."

"Yeah. And?"

"And you're going home ... *Now*." He reached for my hand once again, pulling me forward until I stopped dead in my tracks.

"Just wait a doggone minute! I'm not going anywhere. Besides, I'm not here alone."

"I'm sure Krissy can get home on her own."

"That's not the point," I argued. "I came with her, and I can't just leave without telling her. Hold up ... How do you know her name is Krissy?"

Before he could answer, Krissy came rushing past us and waved. "Don't worry about me, sweetie. I've got a ride. You two kids have fun!"

With a big, goofy smirk on her face, my best friend disappeared out the front door, leaving me alone to deal with Zander. Clearly amused by the fact, he cocked his eyebrow and said, "Well, how about that? Looks like Krissy is covered."

"Yeah, well, no thanks to you." I wanted to stay mad at him. I needed to. It was the only way I could overcome the disappointment I'd felt over not hearing from him for the past two days, but it wasn't easy, especially when he looked so damn good. I crossed my arms in defiance as I snapped, "Why are you here, Zander?"

"You know why."

"I wouldn't be asking if I did."

"I'm here for you." Even though he'd already proven otherwise, he stared at me like I meant something to him —like I was *his*. "I'm taking you home."

With that, he took hold of my hand, and this time I didn't resist as he led me out of the bar and into a crowd of people. When he turned down a dark alley, I thought he was taking me to his bike. Instead, he pinned me up against the wall with his mouth just inches from my ear. The bristles of his day-old beard prickled against my cheek as he whispered, "Why didn't you answer my message?"

"I didn't know it was you."

"Don't lie to me, Delilah," he growled. "Why didn't you answer me?"

"I don't know."

"Yes, you do." He inched closer, and I could feel his growing erection as he ordered, *"Tell me."*

"I wanted to piss you off ... make you pay for blowing me off."

He stepped back and looked at me in surprise. "Blowing you off?"

"Don't stand there and try to deny it. You screwed me and then disappeared, Zander." I wanted to stay mad at him, but it was almost impossible with the way he was looking at me. *"That's blowing me off*, which is fine. I'm a big girl. I can take it."

"It ever cross your mind that I had shit going on?"

"It ever cross your mind to pick up a phone and tell me you had shit going on? It would've taken what ... two seconds of your time." I cocked my eyebrow as I took a step towards him. "So, why bother coming here now? What's so important that you had to come down here and find me?"

"Fuck." He ran his hand through his tousled dark hair. "Are you always such a pain in the ass?"

"No." A smile crept over my face as I admitted, "Just when it comes to you. I guess you could say you bring it out in me."

Before I could say anything more, he slammed his mouth against mine, silencing me with a kiss that set my soul on fire. It was then that I knew I was in trouble. I was falling for him, and there was nothing I could do to stop it.

HAWK

Delilah Davenport challenged me at every turn. She called me out on my bullshit, not letting me get away with anything, and I couldn't deny that it was one of the things that drew me to her. Call me crazy, but I actually liked the fact that she had a stubborn streak a mile long and stood up for what she believed. After spending a second night tangled in Delilah's arms, I thought my feelings about her might change, that I'd finally get her out of my system, but that didn't happen. As luck would have it, as soon as I woke up the next morning, I found myself wanting to have her once again, and something in my gut told me it was a feeling that wasn't going to change any time soon. Even though I hated the idea of getting out of that bed with her, I didn't have a choice. The brothers and I would be leaving in less than an hour for a meet we'd set up between Danny and his handler in Texarkana, and I couldn't be late. I eased out of bed, and as I started to get dressed, Delilah rolled over to face me. "Going somewhere?"

"I've got some club business to take care of."

"But the sun is barely up."

"I'm well aware. I've gotta go just the same."

"Is it really club business, or are you just making up an excuse to leave?"

"I don't make excuses, Delilah. Not for anyone."

"Okay, just checking." She eased up on her elbow. "Does this club business have anything to do with Danny?"

"I've gotta go." I slipped on my cut, then walked over and kissed her on the forehead. "I'll be back late tonight."

"Will I see you?"

"Probably not. Like I said, it'll be late when I get back."

"Okay, be careful."

"Always."

It wasn't easy, especially with her looking so fucking beautiful lying in that bed, but I managed to force myself to walk out of her bedroom and out of her apartment. I got on my bike, and as I drove to the clubhouse, I thought back to the night before when Menace brought to my attention that Delilah had gone down to Music Row with her best friend. Her night out might've gone unnoticed if we hadn't been tracking her phone. When he first told me, I played it off like it was no big deal. I didn't want to admit to him or myself that I was bothered by the fact, but in truth, I was. At the time, I had no intentions of doing anything about it, but the more I thought about her being in that bar, partying with her little buddy, the more aggravated I became. Out of simple frustration, I sent her a text. When I got no response, I went to see for myself what the hell she was up to. I told myself I just wanted to make sure she wasn't putting the club at risk by drinking and revealing the truth about her brother's whereabouts, but I knew that wasn't it. She knew it, too, and she called me out on it—not only at the bar but when we got back to her place.

We were both in the heat of the moment, kissing and rushing to get out of our clothes, and all I could think about was being inside her again, when she stopped me dead in my tracks. "Why did you really come looking for me tonight?"

"You know why."

"Tell me."

I looked down at Delilah, relishing her lust-filled eyes, and I couldn't imagine wanting a woman more. Even though I wanted to tell her the truth, I couldn't. "I was doing my job."

"That's not the only reason, and you know it."

My memory of our exchange was cut short when I pulled through the gate and found Axel outside talking with Viper. As soon as I was parked, I went over and asked, "Is everything still going down as planned?"

"Yeah. We're planning to head out soon," Axel answered. "Where you been?"

"I had some business to tend to."

A smirk crossed his face. "Your business have something to do with your girl being out partying last night?"

"Menace has a big fucking mouth."

"I'll take that as a yes."

Concern crossed Viper's face as he warned, "This isn't the time for distractions, brother."

"It's been taken care of."

"Good to hear." When Shotgun came out with Danny in tow, Viper started walking towards the SUV. "Let's get this thing done."

It was a seven-hour drive to Texarkana, so it was no

surprise that Viper was eager to get on the road. In order to avoid any unwanted suspicions, we'd gone by Danny's place earlier and picked up his car. Shotgun and Danny got in it. With Widow driving, Viper, Axel, Menace, and I followed close behind as they pulled through the gate and out onto the main road. The guys were quiet as we made our way to the interstate, and they remained silent as we crossed the Tennessee state line into Arkansas, giving me time to get lost in my thoughts once again. I found myself thinking of the moment when Delilah had pushed me to tell her the real reason why I'd shown up at the bar. I never actually said the words. Instead, I kissed her, hoping that and what followed would be enough of an answer for her, and it was—at least for the time being. I had a feeling that she would push me to my limits at every turn, but it wasn't something I couldn't handle. This thing with her might be new terrain for me, but she'd learn soon enough that I was a man who could only be pushed so far.

My focus was drawn back to the brothers when Widow asked, "So, when we get this guy back to Nashville, what do you think he's gonna say? I mean ... you really think he's the one who's behind all this bullshit, or are we gonna have to take it a step further?"

"Won't know until Shotgun has a go with him."

Viper was right. We had no idea what the days ahead would hold until we got this guy to talk, and I had a feeling it was going to take some real persuasion on Shotgun's part to get him to tell us exactly what had gone down, especially knowing what was coming to him the second he opened his mouth. Either we'd kill him for swindling us, or his distributor would feed him his balls for ratting him out. The guy was in a no-win situation, and while that might make it more difficult for Shotgun to get him talking, none of us were worried. We all knew he'd do whatever it took to get the information we needed.

When we got closer to the meet location, Shotgun pulled the car over and got in the SUV with us. Danny was wired so we could listen to every word that was said between him and Miller. Menace had also set him up with an earpiece, in case we needed to intervene. As soon as Danny pulled off, Menace got on his mic and warned, "Don't try anything stupid. Make the exchange and leave everything else to us. Understood?"

"Understood."

We followed him a mile down the road, and when he turned off down a deserted road, Widow eased back, giving some distance between our vehicles. As planned, Danny drove behind the old, abandoned Whistle Stop and Go car wash and parked. As we drove by, we noticed a thick wooded area directly behind the car wash—a perfect place for us to hide out during the exchange. Once we were certain Danny was in position, we drove several blocks down the street and parked the SUV behind an empty warehouse. Knowing we didn't have much time, we quickly got out and headed towards the woods, making sure we were close enough to make our move but far enough to not be seen. We'd just gotten settled, when a black Mercedes pulled up to Danny. Danny got out of the car, and as he approached the Mercedes, he was greeted by a tall Hispanic male with long black hair and a thick, burly beard. Listening through his wire, we heard the man ask, "What the fuck happened to you?"

None of us were surprised by the question. While we'd

done our best to clean Danny up, he was still covered in cuts and bruises, and with all the punctures from the ice picks, he was moving a little slow. Thankfully, Danny was quick on his feet. "I made a move on the wrong girl at a bar the other night."

"She teach you a lesson?" Miller scoffed.

"No, but her boyfriend and his buddies sure did. Beat the fuck out of me, but the girl was hot. I had to at least try and get a piece of that."

"Mmm … No lay is worth that shit." Miller's tone quickly changed as he asked, "You got the money?"

"You know I do." Danny reached into his back pocket and pulled out the envelope of cash we'd given him for the exchange. "You got the goods?"

"Yeah, it's in the back." Miller strolled to the rear of the car and nonchalantly opened the trunk. "It's all there."

Like he'd done it a million times before, Danny took out his pocketknife and cut one of the bags, quickly sampling the take. After several moments, he turned his attention to Miller and asked, "The others just like this one?"

"Yeah, why the fuck wouldn't they be?"

"Just checking, man." Danny shrugged. "I don't want any trouble with my buyers. They're the kind of guys who'll string you up by the balls just for shits and giggles."

"They have an issue with the last shipment?"

"No … at least, not that I'm aware of."

Danny was digging a hole, and if he didn't watch his step, he was gonna fuck up everything. Hoping to get him back on track, Menace used his mic and told Danny, "Stop running your fucking mouth and get this thing done."

Miller stood silent, studying Danny's expression, then grumbled, "You want the shit or not?"

"Yeah, yeah, I want it."

When Danny reached into the trunk and started to unload, the guy followed suit. Their attention was on transferring the shipment, so Shotgun gave the nod, letting us know it was time to get a move on. We each followed as Shotgun led us out of hiding and into the abandoned parking lot. As we got closer, I could feel the adrenaline coursing through my veins, bringing every nerve in my body to life—not out of fear, but out of eagerness. I, like the rest of my brothers, wanted to take this motherfucker down, find out exactly what he knew, and get this bullshit over and done with once and for all. Unaware that we were inching closer, Danny and Miller continued to move the product from the Mercedes' trunk over to Danny's. All was going as planned until the sound of a car driving by off in the distance caught Miller's attention. He glanced over his shoulder, and his face grew pale with fear when he saw us advancing towards them. Hell, by looking at his frightened expression one would've thought the guy was watching a pack of angry wolves charging towards him. I couldn't blame him for being rattled. Seeing the five of us in our leather cuts, muscular builds, and tattoos would make any man uneasy. We were just a few yards away when he reached for his revolver and aimed it in our direction. "Who the fuck are you?"

Viper continued to charge forward, completely unfazed by the fact that the barrel of Miller's gun was pointed directly at him. Miller's hand started to tremble with apprehension as he placed his finger on the trigger. "Stop right there or I'll blow your fucking head off."

Hoping to diffuse the situation, Danny looked over to him and started stammering, "Hey, man. I-It's cool. I know these guys. They're business associates of mine."

"What the fuck are you talking about?"

"They just want to ask you a few questions."

"I ain't answering a goddamn thing! Not now. Not ever."

Concerned for Viper's safety, Shotgun and I stepped in front of Viper, shielding his body with ours as Viper warned, "Put the gun down."

"That shit ain't gonna happen, motherfucker."

"Have it your way."

Viper pulled out his Glock, then everyone else did the same. Miller's eyes widened, leaving no doubt that he was intimidated by the sight of all of us standing in front of him with our weapons drawn. Danny's knees were practically shaking, making it more than evident that he was equally as freaked when he started yammering, "Look guys. It doesn't have to go down like this. We all just need to calm the fuck down."

"You got any idea how bad you've fucked this thing up?" Miller asked Danny. "Your ass is gonna be on the line for this shit. It's all gonna come back on you. Wait and see."

"Wouldn't have come to this if you hadn't fucked with the last shipment."

Miller was getting more anxious by the second. He was barely able to keep his grip on his weapon as he barked, "Got no idea what the fuck you're talking about."

"We think you do," Viper growled.

"I'm done with this shit."

The guy's arm stiffened, and there was no doubt he

was about to pull the trigger when Danny lunged in front of him, taking a bullet to the shoulder. As Danny collapsed to the ground, I fired off a round, shooting Miller in the hand. Miller immediately dropped his weapon and started shouting a stream of curses as he cradled his hand to his chest. "Motherfucker!"

I charged over to Miller, placing my gun to the asshole's head, then looked down at his hand and snickered. "That's gotta hurt like a bitch."

"Fuck you, asshole."

"Better watch yourself," Widow warned. "He's not a man you're gonna wanna piss off any more than you already have."

Miller looked up at me, noting the fierce expression on my face, and said nothing more. In fact, he was completely silent as Shotgun and I dragged him over to the Mercedes and locked him in the trunk. Once he was detained, Viper turned his attention to Danny. He knelt down beside him as he asked, "There a reason why you pulled that stunt?"

"He was gonna shoot you," Danny muttered with a grimace. "Figured I'd do what I could to stop him."

"I see." Viper's brows furrowed as he pulled back Danny's t-shirt and studied his wound. "Looks like he got you pretty good."

"Yes, sir, but I'll be all right." Danny glanced over at Shotgun as he admitted, "Those fucking ice pics hurt worse than this."

"Somehow I doubt that," Shotgun replied.

Viper stood and extended his hand to Danny's good arm. "We need to get you back to the clubhouse so Doc can tend to this wound."

Menace and I went over and helped Viper get Danny to his feet, and once we had him loaded into the SUV, I grabbed a towel from the back and offered it to him. "You're gonna need to keep pressure on it. We've got a long drive back to Nashville."

"Thanks, man."

Danny took the towel and pressed it against his shoulder as he leaned his head against the window. It was clear the guy was hurting, but he didn't breathe a single complaint. Instead, he sat silently as we prepared to leave. Menace got in Danny's car, and Shotgun and Widow got in the Mercedes. Once they were set, Viper and I loaded up in the SUV with Danny, and we started back towards Nashville. We hadn't been driving long when I glanced back at Danny. The towel in his hand was almost soaked through with blood, and his complexion was becoming paler by the second. He was struggling, even more than he had under Shotgun's handy work. Considering what he'd put him through, it was hard to believe that he'd taken a bullet for us. The guy definitely had balls, just like his sister. The thought had my mind drifting to Delilah. I had no doubt she'd lose it if she knew her brother had been shot. While it wasn't news I could share with her, there was a possible silver lining to it all. By taking that bullet, Danny might've taken the first step in getting his life back —but he'd have to survive first.

DELILAH

Delilah

I'd just gotten dressed for work when I heard a knock at my door. I couldn't deny that I was hoping it might be Hawk returning, but when I opened it, I found my mother standing in the hallway. She looked like she'd just come from the gym in her sweats and loose t-shirt. Her hair was pulled up, and she was wearing just a hint of makeup and a smile. "Good morning, sweetheart."

"What are you doing here so early?"

"I thought I'd bring breakfast for you and Krissy." She stepped inside my apartment as she continued, "I brought all your favorites."

"That was sweet of you to come all this way."

"Well, I was in the area." A solemn look crossed her face as she admitted, "I went by your brother's place to see if he was home. I was thinking I might be able to catch him if I went by there early."

Already knowing the answer, I asked, "Did you have any luck?"

"No. He wasn't there." She placed the box of donuts on the counter as she sighed. "What about you? Have you had any luck reaching him?"

"Afraid not." I shrugged. "I guess he's still out doing whatever it is he's doing."

"Maybe it's time we contacted the police and filed a missing person's report or something."

"No! I-ah ... I don't think that's a good idea." If I didn't already know where Danny was, I would've insisted that she go to the police, but under the circumstances, I couldn't let that happen. "You know how Danny is. Like I told you before, he's probably just laid up somewhere with a few of his buddies."

"No." She shook her head. "He's in trouble, Dee."

"You can't know that for sure."

"Yes, I can. I'm his mother. I can feel it in my bones." It made my chest ache to see the worried look on her face as she added, "And it's all my fault."

"What are you talking about?"

"I should've done more for him. He needed a father in his life. You both did." Tears filled her eyes as she muttered, "Maybe if I'd stayed with your father ..."

"Mom, stop," I fussed. "You staying with Dad wouldn't have been good for any of us, and you know it."

"I don't know that, Delilah." I could see the wheels turning in her head as she leaned back against the counter and crossed her arms. "I know you may not remember, especially after the way things played out, but there was a lot of good in your father. I can still remember when I first fell in love with him. He was so handsome and charming and funny. Oh, my ... the way we used to laugh." Her eyes drifted to the floor as she continued, "He would give the best hugs. Made me feel like I was truly loved ... and he was great with you and your brother. You both were always crawling onto his lap, listening to him tell one story after the next."

"You're right. I don't remember that." I came off harsher than I intended when I said, "I remember the yelling ... and all the times the lights would get turned off because he'd gambled away all your money. I remember him being gone for days on end and how worried you were that he might not come home. But he always did, and when he finally did show up, it was only because he'd ran out of money."

"He was sick, Delilah. It wasn't his fault."

"His fault or not, he caused more harm than good."

"Maybe things could've been different if I'd pushed him harder to get help."

"What is it with you and the blame game?" I fussed. "It wasn't your job to make Dad do right by his family and get the help he needed. If he cared at all, he would've gotten the help on his own. He certainly wouldn't have entirely given up on us all."

"I guess you're right."

"I'm definitely right." I gave her a warm smile as I tried to assure her, "Besides, we did just fine without him. You were a wonderful mother. You still are."

"It's just so hard to be sure." She wiped the tears from her cheek as she explained, "A boy needs a man in his life that he can look up to and respect. Danny never had that."

"No, but he had you. That's all either of us really needed." I walked over to her and gave her a hug. "Everything's going to be okay. You'll see."

"I hope you're right about that." She stepped back with a look of doubt on her face. "Are you sure we shouldn't contact the police ... just to be certain?"

"No. I honestly think it's best to wait." Hoping to buy myself some time, I offered, "How about this? I'll go by his place after work, and if he's not there, I'll make some calls and see if I can track him down?"

"That would be great."

"Okay, consider it done."

"Thank you, sweetheart." She gave me a quick hug before saying, "I'll let you finish getting ready for work."

Once she was gone, I grabbed my things, along with the donuts my mother had brought, and rushed to work. As soon as I walked into the nursing home, I dropped Mom's donuts off in the work room, and after I put my things in my locker, I headed out to do my rounds. I hadn't been at it long when my mind drifted to my conversation with my mother. It had been years since she'd talked about my father, and I was surprised that she had anything positive to say about him. He'd caused us all so much heartache, and as far as I knew, he'd never tried to set things right. Not that it mattered. I found it doubtful that I would ever be able to forgive him for the things he'd done. I wished I could. It would be nice to finally let go of all that anger and resentment, but it was just too hard. Maybe in time I'd see things differently, but for the time being, it was easier to blame him for the things that had gone wrong in our lives—including Danny's ordeal with the Ruthless Sinners. Maybe if my father had been around, then Danny wouldn't have taken to dealing drugs. It was a thought that had me thinking about Zander.

I'd always promised myself that I wouldn't make the same mistakes my mother had made with my father. I didn't want to spend my life constantly looking over my shoulder or waiting for the next bomb to drop like my mother had. I wanted a man who'd be honest and good—a man who'd love me and always be there when I needed them. I wasn't sure where exactly Zander fit in that promise I'd made to myself. Every instinct I had screamed at me to walk away, but my heart just wouldn't listen. I knew he was involved in bad things. I'd seen that with my own eyes, but I also knew there was another side to him—a good side. I'd seen it, *felt it*, but deep down, I wasn't sure it was enough. I was still trying to wrap my head around it all when Krissy snuck up behind me and asked, "Well?"

I glanced over my shoulder and found her standing behind me with a big goofy smile spread across her face. Even though I knew she wanted to know what happened after she'd left the bar, I feigned ignorance. "Well, what?"

"You know what! How did it go with your guy last night?"

"It went okay. More than okay." I couldn't help but smile as I said, "I think we got things sorted or, at least, partly sorted."

"So, my girl got laid again." She teased. "I couldn't be happier for you."

"Don't get too excited. I'm not sure if I'll be seeing him again."

"What? Why not?"

"I don't know. I'm just scared, I guess." I shrugged with

doubt. "I don't want to end up with a broken heart."

"There's always that chance with any guy, Dee, but I gotta tell ya"—her smile suddenly faded—"I'd give anything to have a guy look at me the way he was looking at you last night. Damn. He's got it bad for you, girl, and if I didn't know better, I'd say you felt the same way about him."

I wasn't sure I was ready to admit it to her or myself, but she was right. Right or wrong, I was falling for Zander. There was something about him that got to me in a way no man ever had, and it terrified me. There was no way I could explain it all to Krissy, so I decided to try and change the subject. "What about you and your guy from last night? Did you have a good time?"

"He was all right, I guess. He seemed like a nice guy and all, but there were no fireworks or anything." A look of indifference crossed her face as she chuckled. "I don't think he's the one, but I'll go out with him again just to be sure."

"You'll have to let me know how that goes."

"I will, and I expect you to do the same with your fella. I think you might be surprised by how things will play out between you two."

"We'll see." There was a commotion in one of the resident's rooms down the hall, so I used the opportunity to cut our conversation short. "I better get down to Mrs. Williams' room and see how she's doing."

"Okay." When I turned to leave, she called out, "I'll be expecting an update soon."

"I know you will!"

After I checked in with Mrs. Williams, I spent the rest of my day staying busy with rounds and paperwork. By the time I made it back home, I was exhausted, but that didn't stop me from checking my window every few minutes for any sign of Zander or his brothers in my parking lot. When I wasn't checking my window, I was glancing down at my phone, hoping that by some chance I might actually hear from him before I went to bed. Unfortunately, that didn't happen. I knew he said he would be gone for the day, but I was hoping that he might touch base with me, especially after our little discussion the night before.

After hours of foolishly waiting and hoping, I finally gave up and went to bed. Consumed with frustration, I tossed and turned for hours, questioning over and over whether I should simply end things with him and relieve myself of the constant fretting. Even though it might've been easier, the thought didn't set well with me. In fact, the mere thought of never seeing him again made my heart ache with dread.

I don't know how long I'd been lying there when I finally gave in to my exhaustion and drifted off to sleep. I was in the thick haze of sleep when I heard a strange sound in my bathroom. I sat up in my bed, listening in utter fright as the noise became louder and louder, followed by the sound of water coming from the shower. While I was scared out of my mind, I found it doubtful that an intruder would take a shower before slicing my throat, so I eased out of bed and crept over to the bathroom door. My hand trembled as I turned the doorknob and stepped inside. My breath caught in my throat when I found a naked Zander standing in my shower in all his wondrous glory. The water trickled down his chest as he smiled and said, "Hey ... I thought you were sleeping."

"I was." I tried to keep my eyes from roaming south as I placed my hands on my hips and let out a huff. "What are you doing here?"

"I'm taking a shower."

"I see that, Zander. How did you get in here?"

A sexy smirk crossed his face as he replied, "You're not the only one who can pick a lock, darlin'."

"You picked my lock?"

"Well, yeah. I didn't want to hear your mouthin' again about me blowing you off."

"So, you broke into my apartment?" I gasped. "Do you have some kind of aversion to picking up a phone?"

Without a response, he reached out and grabbed my hand, pulling me into the shower with him. My t-shirt quickly became soaked under the stream of water, along with the rest of me, but I didn't mind. Being close to him set my entire body on fire with need. His eyes were filled with desire. "What can I say? I needed to see you."

Damn. I loved that look in his eyes—like he'd never get enough of me. Zander's hands slipped around my waist as he leaned towards me and pressed his lips firmly against mine. The kiss was hungry and full of want as he pulled me closer. I wound my arms around his neck while his calloused fingertips roamed down the small of my back. When he touched me, it was just him and me, making me forget about everything else—the doubts, the chaos, and guilt faded into nothing. A soft whimper escaped my lips as he lifted my wet t-shirt over my head, tossing it to the shower floor.

Water cascaded down our bodies as his hand trailed down to my thighs, easing my panties down to my ankles. Once they were gone, he lifted me up, and in a blink, my back was pressed against the cold, wet tile. Seeking more, I tilted my head back, letting the water flow down my breasts. He trailed kisses along the curve of my neck to my collarbone, and ever so slowly, he moved one of his hands up and down my slick side. His fingers brushed against my breasts and then down to my hips, and I groaned with pleasure as his hand found its way between my legs. His fingers slipped inside me, moving ever so gently as he said, "You're so fucking beautiful."

"Zander."

"Do you have any idea what you do to me?"

"Tell me." I gasped as he moved faster inside me.

"I haven't been able to get you out of my head. I can't stop thinking about all the things I'm going to do to you ... all the different ways I'm going to make you come." He lowered his mouth to my neck, and as he trailed kisses down my shoulder, he whispered, "You're mine, Delilah ... every fucking inch of you."

Hearing him claim me in such a primal way sent me over the edge. My hips jolted forward as my body clenched firmly around his fingers. I was floating on the high of my release, relishing the moment of ecstasy, when he lowered himself down to his knees. His mouth came closer, and with one flick of his tongue, my entire body was consumed with desire. My hands dove into Zander's hair as I shamelessly pulled him closer. I'd never been so turned on, and he had just gotten started. What began in the shower moved into the bedroom, where he spent the entire night exploring every inch of my body.

By the time he was done, we were both exhausted and wondrously sated and collapsed on the bed. He rested his head on the pillow as I curled into his side, my head in the crook of his arm. We lay there motionless for several minutes, trying to catch our breath. I'm not sure what spurred the thought, maybe it was feeling the connection between us growing stronger, or maybe I just needed him to know how I felt. Either way, I looked up at him. "Can I tell you something?"

"Um-hmm."

I propped up on my elbow, so I could look at him as I said, "I don't know what this thing is that's happening between us, and to be honest, I'm not sure I want to know ... but I like it. I'm really happy when I'm with you."

His voice was soft and low as he whispered, "Delilah."

"You don't have to say anything. I'm not asking for some kind of declaration or anything. I just wanted you to know how I felt."

He didn't respond. I didn't expect him to. I closed my eyes as I listened to the relaxing rhythm of his heartbeat, and even though I tried to fight it, I drifted off to sleep. I woke up the next morning in an empty bed with a note from Zander on my pillow, letting me know he'd gone to back to the clubhouse. I was disappointed but not surprised, as I crawled out of bed and headed to the shower. By the time I was out and dressed, it was almost noon. I didn't have to go into work, so I made myself busy by cleaning up my apartment and doing laundry. Once I was done, I crawled up on the sofa and turned on the TV. A smile spread across my face when I saw that a rerun of *Animal Kingdom* was on. It made me think back to the night I'd invited Zander up to my apartment. At the time, I hadn't realized that our dinner together would be the start of something more—maybe that was what I'd hoped for all along.

HAWK

"I gotta say, that motherfucker has balls," Rafe announced. It had only been a few days since he'd been shot, but he wasn't the kind of man who'd let a couple of bullet wounds slow him down. His shoulder was up in a sling and he was moving a little slower than usual, but Rafe looked like he was holding his own as he stood outside of one of Shotgun's rooms. Miller's tortured cries were penetrating into the hallway as Shotgun continued to work him over, and a mischievous smile crossed his face as Rafe motioned his head towards the door. "Well, at least he had 'em. After that round of screaming I just heard, I'm not so sure anymore."

"I take it Miller's not talking?"

"Fuck no, but from the sounds of it, he'll be singing like a canary before long."

"I hope you're right about that."

"Me, too." He shook his head. "I don't know if I can stomach much more of this shit."

"Rough in there?"

"Fuck, yeah. Dude looks like he's been through a fucking meat grinder. Turns my stomach just thinking about it." A pained expression crossed Rafe's face as he continued, "Hell, I would've started spilling it the second I saw Shotgun coming at me with a fucking sledge hammer, but this guy's being all stubborn and shit. He hasn't said a fucking word about what went down with the take."

"Gotta wonder why he's trying so hard to keep it under wraps."

"I was thinking the same fucking thing."

The screams continued, and I was considering going in to check on things when Viper and Axel walked up. I figured they were like me and eager to find out if Shotgun had managed to get him to talk, and I had no doubt that they'd both be just as disappointed as I was that Miller still hadn't. Viper turned to me as he asked, "Anything?"

"Not a word."

"Fuck," he grumbled. "I'm about fed up with this bullshit."

"I'm sure Shotgun feels the same. He's been at it all fucking night."

"I think I've got something that might help," Menace interrupted as he come rushing up the hall. As he offered Viper a folder, he told him, "Here's the information you wanted on Miller."

Viper opened the folder, and after reading it over for a moment, he said, "It's time to put an end to this shit once and for all."

Without a moment's hesitation he reached for the doorknob, and as he opened it, we were all hit with a foul odor of vomit mixed with shit. It was enough to turn my stomach, but the smell was nothing compared to the sight of Miller. Much like Danny, he was strung up with his hands over his head, but he was sitting with his feet bound to the legs of a chair. I had to fight back my gag reflexes as I looked down at his bare feet and shins. They were all broken and mangled from where Shotgun had worked him over with the sledgehammer, and I found it doubtful that Miller would ever walk again. His face was barely recognizable, and I was surprised that the guy was not only conscious but seemed completely aware of his surroundings. Viper grabbed a chair from the corner and took it over to Miller. As he sat down in front of him, he open the folder and said, "Scott Miller. Son of Donna and Hamilton Miller. 129 Tigrett Street, Texarkana, Arkansas. Age thirty-four."

"Yeah...so?"

"Nicole Miller. Daughter of Scott Miller. Age seven. Living at ..."

Before Viper could finish, Miller spat, "What the fuck does my daughter have to do with this shit?"

"That is entirely up to you." Viper held up the folder, showing Miller the picture Menace found of his daughter. "Cute kid. Sure would hate to see anything happen to her."

"Look here, motherfucker. If you lay one finger on her, I'll kill you! I'll kill every last fucking one of you!" Miller barked, making it clear Viper had hit a nerve.

"I think we both know you're in no position to make threats, so why don't you just save us both some trouble and tell us what we want to know." Viper closed the folder and leaned back in his chair. "Otherwise, me and my boys are gonna make another trip to Arkansas, and that sweet little girl of yours is going to find out what monsters are really made of."

"Fuck you!"

"All right, then. *Have it your way.*"

Viper stood, and when he started towards the door, Miller shouted, "It was me. I'm the one who did it."

"Any particular reason why it was our shipment you decided to fuck with?"

"I didn't know it was yours. I just get the orders and fill 'em. I figured since it was such a big take, no one would be the wiser."

"You thought we wouldn't notice that over half of it was fucking trash?" Viper went over and reached for his throat, gripping it tightly as he growled, "The Ruthless Sinners don't deal fucking trash, asshole. Not now. Not ever."

Miller's face was turning red from the lack of oxygen and he was close to passing out when Viper finally released him. Miller gasped for breath as he stammered, "I-I get that. I really do, but it's done now. It's not like I can take it back."

"You're right about that." Viper stood over him, scowling as he studied him, then he turned and looked at us. I could see the wheels turning in his head, but I had no idea what he was thinking. After several, long moments, Viper walked back over to the chair in front of Miller and sat down. As he lean forward, glaring at Miller, he cocked his head and said, "You know ... something's just not adding up with all this."

"What are you talking about?" Miller asked, sounding innocent. "I told you everything."

Viper shook his head as he grumbled, "I'm not buying it."

"I don't know what else to tell ya, man. It was me."

"Okay, then why all the bullshit." Viper cocked his head to the side as he said, "Why not just fess up to it in the beginning?"

"It doesn't matter," Miller told him. "You know the truth. That's all you need to know."

"I'm the one who decides what the fuck I need to know. Not you, asshole, so cut the bullshit!" Even though I was standing several feet away, I could feel the anger radiating off Viper as he growled, "I know you got a reason for putting yourself through all this shit, and you've got two seconds to tell me what the fuck it is or I'm going to get that daughter of yours and—"

"Don't!" Miller pleaded. "I'll tell you what you want to know."

"I'm listening."

"You gotta understand ... You finding out what I did is one thing. I know it's bad, *really bad*, and you're pissed that I swindled ya. Hell, I know I'm not walking outta here alive"—a troubled look crossed Miller's face as he sat there staring back at Viper—"but the boss ... *Fuck*. If he finds out that I fucked with his product, that I put his distribution line in jeopardy, then it won't just be me who goes down for it. My whole fucking family will burn for my mistake. I wasn't gonna let that happen."

"Too late."

"What the fuck you talking about?"

"When you don't show up with his cash, where do you

think that boss of yours is gonna go first?" Miller's face grew pale as the realization of what he'd done finally sank in. "You fucked up big, kid, and you've got no one to blame but yourself."

Viper stood up, and as he started towards the door, Miller said, "You know my boss is a smart guy."

"And?"

"When he puts two and two together, he'll come looking for you, and when that happens, you'll all go down. Every last one of ya."

"And that's why we have Billy," Viper replied with confidence. "He'll see to it that *that* doesn't happen."

Then, Viper turned and started for the door. We had the answers we'd been looking for, so our time with Miller was done. We all knew once Viper brought in Billy the Butcher, he'd see to it that Miller paid the final penance for his crimes against the club. Menace, Axel, and I followed Viper out of the room and into the hall. When the door closed behind us, Axel shook his head and said, "Dumb kid's got no idea what a fucking mess he's made."

"No, he doesn't."

I knew Billy was good. Hell, he was the best around. That's why we used him, but this wasn't just a simple clean up. He would have to make sure no unwanted repercussions fell back on us, and considering everything that had gone down, that wouldn't be easy. "You think Billy can keep this thing from coming back on us?"

Viper ran his hand over his beard as he said, "He's going to have to. One way or another, we've gotta see to it that there's no blowback from any of this. Last thing we need is some fucking drug boss thinking we fucked him over ... took out one of his guys and stole one of his shipments."

"Yeah, losing a handler is one thing," Axel replied. "Losing ten grand is another."

"Maybe Billy can make it look like Miller split with the cash or something?" Menace suggested. "His boss has gotta know that he was delivering another order."

"Maybe so." Viper took his phone out of his pocket as he said, "I'll get with Billy and go from there. I trust him to handle it."

Before he made the call, Axel asked, "You need anything from us?"

"Get with some of the guys, and go over and check on the remodel at the new club. I want us opening as soon as possible." Then, he turned to me and Menace. "You two stick around in case Billy needs a hand with something."

"You got it," Menace answered. "Let us know when he gets here."

"You know I will."

When Viper started down the hall to make his call to Billy the Butcher, Axel went to gather up the others, and Menace headed down his room to wait for Billy's arrival. Since I had some time on my hands, I decided to go check in on Danny. I hadn't thought to ask the others how he was doing, so I decided to go see for myself. When I got down to the infirmary, I found Danny in the room alone. He was lying on one of the gurneys with an IV stuck in his arm. At first look, I thought he was asleep, but as I entered farther into the room, he turned to look at me. "You here to finish me off?"

"Not exactly," I scoffed. "Just wanted to see how you were doing."

"I've been better, but this sure beats being in that room with that friend of yours."

"I'm sure it does."

"You find out what you needed to know from Miller?"

"That's not something up for discussion."

"What about my sister?" A hopeful look crossed his face as he asked, "Can you at least tell me if she's okay?"

If the guy hadn't taken a bullet for us, I wouldn't have felt inclined to tell him a fucking thing, but since he'd risked his life, I decided to ease his mind a little. "She's fine."

"You still keeping her here?"

"We released her, but we've been keeping an eye on her."

"You know she didn't have anything to do with all this. Hell, she didn't even know I was dealing."

"Yeah." I nodded. "I'm aware of that."

"Not sure she'll ever forgive me for putting her in danger."

"I don't know. Your sister seems to have a soft spot where you're concerned."

"Oh really?" His brows furrowed with confusion. "What makes you say that?"

"Just a hunch."

"I don't know." He studied me for a moment, then replied, "Something tells me there's more to it than just a hunch."

"Seems to me that you need to be less concerned about my hunches, and more concerned about what's going to happen to you now."

"Like I told Delilah, I'm not expecting to up and walk

out of here. I made a bad deal, and instead of facing the shit head on, I shot one of your guys."

"I don't disagree. You definitely fucked up, but what you did yesterday with Miller didn't go unnoticed by Viper."

"It's not a big deal. Anyone would've done it."

"I disagree with you there."

"So, maybe there's a chance for me yet ... or do you think he's still set on ending me?"

"You wouldn't be lying here hooked up to this IV if there wasn't a chance."

Danny nodded. "Good to know."

"I gotta get going. I'll be back later to see how you're making it."

"Thanks, man. I appreciate that." When I turned and started towards the door, he asked, "When you see Delilah, are you gonna tell her about what happened at the meet?"

As I stood in the doorway, I turned to him and asked, "What makes you think I'll be seeing her?"

"I guess you could call it a hunch."

Even though I knew she'd be pissed that I hadn't told her about her brother being shot, there was nothing I could do about it. Club business was never discussed outside of the club. Period. Whether I liked it or not, I had no choice but to keep what happened under wraps. Before I walked out, I looked him dead in the eye and said, "No, I won't be telling her anything, and if you're smart, you'll do the same."

When I left there, I went down to the kitchen for some coffee and a quick bite to eat. Sadly, the coffee was long gone, but there were some leftovers in the fridge that I was able to warm up. I'd just finished off the last of the bacon when Menace walked in. "Billy just pulled up."

"That was quick."

"I know. Apparently, he was already in the area."

I got up and followed Menace out to the parking lot. When we got outside, Billy was standing by his van, and like the last time I saw him, he was wearing a pair of slacks with a white button down. His hair was perfectly combed to the side, and his glasses were down on the brim of his nose as he said, "Viper called."

"Yeah, he's waiting for you around back."

He nodded, then went to the back of his van and grabbed his duffle bag. With it in hand, he followed us to the room where we were holding Miller. When we got to the door, Viper was standing there waiting for us. "Appreciate you coming and helping us out like this, Billy."

"That's what I'm here for." His tone was all business as he asked, "So, what exactly are we dealing with today."

Viper took some time to fill Billy in on what had gone down with both Danny and Miller. Once he was done, he casually opened the door, and we all watched as Billy stepped inside. Miller took one look at him in his slacks and dress shirt, then shook his head and chuckled under his breath, making it clear he had no idea what he was in store for. With a smile still plastered on his face, Miller watched Billy drop his duffle bag to the floor, then reach inside for one of his bright orange hazmat suits. Miller's smirk started to fade as Billy stepped inside his suit and zipped it up. After pulling out a large plastic tarp, he looked over to Viper and said, "I'll need him to be standing for this."

"You got it."

Shotgun stepped towards Miller and grabbed the chain over his head, giving it a hard yank and forcing him up. While writhing in agony from standing on his mutilated feet, Shotgun clipped the zip-ties at Miller's ankles. Billy eased forward as he said, "That's good. Leave his hands tied up until I get this done."

Shotgun nodded, then stepped out of Billy's way as he slapped a piece of duct tape over his mouth. Once it was secured, he opened the tarp and started to wrap Miller in it like he was already dead. I had no idea why he was doing that, but considering that he was a genius when it came to this shit, I saw no reason to question his methods. Miller, on the hand, was more than a little rattled by it all. There was no missing the fear in his eyes as Billy covered his face with the plastic.

After he had his body completely covered, he used duct tape to keep the tarp in place. As soon as he was done, he looked over to Viper and said, "Would you mind getting your boys to put him in the van?"

"No problem."

After Shotgun removed the remaining restraints around Miller's wrists, we carried him out to the parking lot and tossed him into Billy's van. After we closed the doors, Billy turned to Viper and said, "I'm going to need his keys."

Viper reached into his pocket for Miller's keys, then handed them over to Billy. "Anything else?"

Billy started to remove his hazmat suit as he answered, "I'll need you to text me the exact time and location of your meet yesterday."

"I can do that. Anything else?"

"Not at the moment." He put his suit into the duffle

bag, then tossed it inside the van. As he got inside, he turned to Viper and said, "I'll contact you when the job is done."

He closed his door, and as he drove away, we thought our troubles with Miller and his drug boss were done.

We were wrong. Very, very wrong.

DELILAH

"You seem quiet." We'd been lying in bed for a half hour or so, and Zander hadn't said more than two words to me. I was starting to think something was wrong. "Do you have something on your mind?"

"No, I'm good." He pulled me over to his side and smiled. "Why? You got a problem with me being *quiet*?"

"Not at all. I'm just not used to it." I cocked my eyebrow as I looked up at him and smiled. "You're usually one to tell me exactly what's on your mind."

"Is that right?" He lowered his mouth to my neck, lightly trailing kisses below my ear. "Well, do I need to tell you what I'm thinking right now?"

"No. I have a pretty good idea." I giggled as I inched away from him. "I was thinking we might get out and do something today."

"Really? Whatcha have in mind?"

"Maybe you could take me out for another ride on your bike?" I'd only been out with him once, and that was just for him to get me back to my car. Even though it was brief, I'd actually enjoyed it—*a lot*. The weather was great, and I thought it would be a nice break for Zander, especially after he'd been working so hard to help the brothers get the new club up and running. "We could pack a lunch and ride out to Radnor Lake. Maybe look around and enjoy the sunshine for a little while, then we can come back here and have a late dinner?"

"Yeah. We could definitely do that, but first ..."

He rolled over on top of me, hovering just a moment as he looked down at me with those gorgeous green eyes. I watched in anticipation as he lowered his mouth to mine, kissing me, soft and tender. My hands drifted to his back, my fingertips slowly roaming before slipping into his hair. A low growl vibrated through his chest as his hand inched its way down my stomach, slipped under the waistband of my lace panties, and continued to drift lower until the tips of his fingers dipped between my thighs and inched towards my center. As my entire body shivered in anticipation, I inhaled a deep, torturous breath and tilted my head back to relish the sensation as he moved his fingers in slow, methodical circles. I was just starting to feel a slight tingling in my stomach when he reached for the hem of my t-shirt and quickly pulled it over my head. He'd barely had a chance to toss it to floor before he was reaching for my panties. As soon as they were gone, Zander was back on top of me, looking down at my naked body like a predator about to consume its prey, causing goosebumps to prickle against my skin. He lowered his mouth to my shoulder and trailed kisses past my collarbone down to my breasts. Heavy breaths and low moans filled the room as he took one of my nipples into his mouth. It felt incredible to be there in his arms, to have his body so close to mine, but I needed more. Eagerly, I rocked my hips forward, back and forth, causing his erection to rake against my warm, wet center. He growled once again, making every nerve in my body hum with need as I ground my clit against him.

"*Fuck*," he groaned as he dug his fingers into my flesh. He turned onto his back, and without releasing his hold on me, pulled me up on top of him to straddle his hips. I looked down at his long, thick shaft, licking my lips as I took him in my hand, slowly stroking him up and down. I could feel him growing harder, and when I couldn't stand it a moment longer, I positioned him at my entrance. With one swift thrust, he slammed deep inside me, giving me every inch of his rock-hard cock. I stilled for a moment, trying to adjust to him before I started to move my hips again. I started slow, relishing feeling him deep inside me, but with every shift of my hips, my body burned for more. Consumed with lust and emotion, I looked at him and with my voice trembling, I whispered, "I've never wanted anyone like I want you."

"You've got me, baby. I'm all yours."

The words had barely left his mouth when he shifted forward, finding that spot that made every nerve in my body tingle. As I looked down at his handsome face, a warmth rushed over me—not the kind of warmth that one might feel in the throes of passion, but the kind that was felt by being with someone special. There was no doubt that I was attracted to Zander. I had been from the first moment I saw him, but as I'd gotten to know him, I'd seen how kind and compassionate he could be, and the attraction I felt for him had grown stronger because of it.

He placed his hands on my hips, guiding me back and forth in a slow, steady rhythm.

Being in his arms made me feel so connected to him, so complete, and I didn't want the moment to end. He continued to guide me in the relentless rhythm he'd set, and with each shift of his hips, I could feel my climax building, burning through my veins.

"Oh, God!" I cried as I tightened around him.

Knowing I was getting close, his movements became rough and demanding as he drove into me deeper and harder. A deep groan resonated through his chest as my orgasm crashed over me, causing my entire body to tense around him. He thrust into me one last time, finally giving in to his own release.

After several minutes, I slowly eased off him and lowered myself to the bed, then pulled me over to him. I rested my head on his chest as I listened to the sounds of our ragged breaths echo throughout the room. Then, the room grew silent, and Zander looked down at me with emotion-filled eyes. "I don't know what it is, but I just ... can't seem to get enough of you."

"Is that a bad thing?"

"No. It's just something I didn't expect." He leaned over and kissed me on the forehead. "I never knew it could be like this."

I eased up on my elbow, looking down at him with a warm smile and whispered, "Don't worry. I'm sure you'll tire of me soon enough."

"Not a chance."

He slipped his arm around me, pulling me close as he kissed me long and hard. Just as he was starting to get me all worked up for a second time, he released me and eased out of bed. "Hey, where are you going?"

"Taking a shower." As he started towards the bathroom, he looked over to me and smiled, "Day light's a wasting."

"You're gonna get me all worked up and just leave me hanging?"

"Come get in the shower with me, and I'll make it up to you."

Without any hesitation, I threw back the covers and followed him into the bathroom. Just as I'd hoped, Zander made good on his word. So good, in fact, the only thing that got us out of the shower was when the water turned cold. After we got dressed, I made a few sandwiches and packed them all up, then we headed down to his bike. After placing our lunch in one of the saddlebags, he offered me a helmet. "You ready?"

"Absolutely."

He kicked his leg over the seat, and once he was settled, offered his hand and helped me climb on behind him. Even though I'd ridden with Zander before, I was still a little nervous, but I knew I'd be safe with him. I placed my hands on his waist and a minute later, we were out on the road. With the warmth of the sun my face and the cool breeze blowing in my hair, I quickly relaxed and was amazed at how free I felt. In fact, being on the back of his bike with his body so close to mine, I felt more like myself than I ever had. We'd been riding for about forty-five minutes or so when I realized we'd arrived at Radnor Lake State Park, and just as I remembered, the views were absolutely incredible. The trees were full of bright green leaves, and all the wildflowers were in bloom. We continued into the park, and it wasn't long before Zander found a spot for us by the water. He pulled over and parked, then we grabbed our lunch and headed over to a small picnic table next to the lake.

Zander smiled as he sat down. "This was a good idea."

"I'm glad you think so." I glanced out at the water and was in complete awe as I watched the sunlight shimmer against the waves. "It's really beautiful here."

"I could say something cheesy, like it's not nearly as beautiful as you, but I'll save us both from that embarrassment."

"I don't know. I kind of like you being cheesy." I giggled as I turned to look at him. "You're usually such a hard-ass. It's nice to know you've got a sweet side."

"There's nothing about me that's sweet, Delilah."

"Hmm ... I think you're wrong, but I'll leave it at that." I glanced back at the water, and out of the blue, I found myself thinking about the last time I'd been out at the lake. It was with my mother and Danny. Much like we were doing today, she'd taken us both out for a picnic, and we spent the entire afternoon playing around the water, skipping rocks, and laughing. The memory brought a sudden tightness my chest, making me miss Danny even more than I already had been. I knew it was doubtful that Zander would open up to me about what was going on with him, but that didn't stop me from turning to him and asking, "How's Danny doing?"

"He's hanging on."

"What exactly does that even mean, Zander?" I pushed. "You're still beating him half-to-death for some stupid drug deal gone bad, but hey... *he's still breathing*. Is that it?

Is that what's going on, or do you mean something else when you say 'he's hanging on'?"

"We've gone over this, Delilah. I can't talk about club business with you." A strange expression crossed his face, making me think he might be trying to hide something as he continued, "I know it's been hard, really hard, but you're just going to have to trust me when I say everything is going to be okay."

It was difficult for me not to push for more, but I knew he'd already said more than he probably should. Besides, there was something in his voice that helped ease the tightness in my chest, so I decided I'd let it go, at least for the time being, and trust that he meant it when he said everything would be okay. I inhaled a deep breath and tried to redirect my thoughts but didn't have much luck. No matter how hard I tried, my mind kept dwelling on Zander and his brothers, so after a few moments, I finally asked him, "How long have you been a member?"

"Of the Sinners?" I nodded. "About thirteen years. Give or take."

"And you like it?"

"Wouldn't be a member if I didn't." His handsome face was void of expression as he told me, "The club life isn't for everyone, Delilah, but for me ... it's been everything. Like I've told you before, those men are my family."

"Those men are dealing drugs, torturing people, and God knows what else. How can you call them family?" When I saw his face twist into a scowl, I knew I'd hit a nerve, but it was difficult for me to understand why a man who'd been so good to me was involved with criminals. I held up my hand, trying to calm him down and said, "Don't get mad. I'm just asking for you to explain it to me ... help me understand."

"I'm not sure there is a way for me to explain that would make you understand."

"Please try."

He turned to look out at the water, seemingly collecting his thoughts and then said, "Don't go thinking I grew up in some broken home or anything. I had a good life. Had good folks, good friends, but I always felt like there was something I was missing. I didn't know what that was until I met the brothers."

"What exactly did you find with them?"

He turned to me, his eyes full of emotion and said, "A sense of belonging ... a wholeness like I'd never felt before. I know it may be hard for you to understand, but the second I walked into the Sinners' clubhouse, I knew it was where I was meant to be. It just felt right, and that feeling hasn't ever changed."

"But if the club is so great, why can't you talk about what goes on there?"

"It's our way of protecting one another, especially our women. The less you know, the safer you'll be." Zander reached out and took my hand in his. "I know you have your reasons for thinking what you do about my brothers and the club, but they're good men. I wouldn't be a member if they weren't."

"I'm trying to comprehend it all, but it's a lot to take in."

"It is, but maybe in time you'll be able to see the club as I do—a place where you know someone will always have your back." His eyes never left mine as he said, "You're mine, so they'll treat you like family and do whatever it takes to protect you. Hell, if it comes down to it, they'll take a bullet for you."

"Okay."

Sensing I was still having doubts, he leaned in and kissed me softly on the forehead. "My brothers aren't like your father, Delilah. They'd never sacrifice your life for their own selfish needs. They just don't work that way. For us, it's all about doing what's best for the entire club, no matter what the circumstances."

It was like he'd read my mind. From the beginning, I was worried that I might be making the same mistakes my mother had made with my father. While I was still a bit skeptical, it gave me hope to hear him say there was a possibility the guys weren't like my father. Zander could tell from my expression that he was finally getting through to me, so he pushed, "If you give them a chance, I guarantee, you won't regret it."

"Okay. I'm not making any promises, but I'll do my best to keep an open mind and give them a chance."

"That's all I'm asking." He reached for the bag of sandwiches and asked, "You hungry?"

"Starving."

We pulled all the food out of the bag and started eating. I took the moment to think about everything Zander had told me about his brothers. It was clear by the way he spoke that he cared a great deal about them, and while I might not understand it all, I hoped in time I would be able to accept the life he'd chosen for himself—otherwise I might lose him. I didn't like the thought of that happening, so I would at least try to give these men a chance. We were almost finished eating when Zander looked over to me and asked, "You never told me ... what made you decide to become a nurse?"

"I don't know. I guess I liked the idea of helping people." I shrugged. "I always thought I'd end up working at one of the hospitals, but I really like it at the nursing home."

"They're lucky to have you."

"I don't know about that, but the residents seems to like me ... at least most days they do."

"McClanahan sure had good things to say about you."

"Oh really? I didn't know he ever said anything nice." I chuckled as I told him, "He's usually pretty ornery, but he sure seemed to like you. I don't think I've ever seen him quite so happy."

"Did you know he used to be the president of the Dark Ravens?"

"The Dark Ravens? I don't think I've ever heard of them."

"They're an older MC. Been around for years." He finished off the last of his soda before saying, "I didn't know who he was when I first walked in, but once I got him to talking, I knew right away. McClanahan was known for being a good leader. He kept his boys in line, and they thrived because of it."

"I had no idea." I suddenly felt very sorry for the man. It couldn't have been easy for him to have led that kind of life only to find himself sitting alone in a nursing home. "It definitely sheds a new light on why he's been so unhappy."

"Yeah. It can't be easy for him." I couldn't help but smile when Zander said, "I'll plan on going by there again this week, and maybe I'll bring one of my brothers along."

"I think he'd like that."

"Good deal." Zander started to gather our things as he said, "You ready to get out of here? Ride for a bit before it gets dark?"

"Absolutely."

As soon as we'd cleaned everything up from our lunch, we got back on Zander's Harley, and a little jolt of excitement surged through me when the engine roared to life. He throttled the ignition, and a smile crossed my face as we drove out of the parking lot. It seemed strange to me that I got such a thrill out of being on his bike. I knew part of it was the fact that I was with Zander. He rode with such confidence and strength, like he was invincible, and I felt completely safe as I nestled up behind him. I'd been to the lake many times before, seen the same views and ridden on the same roads, but on the back of that bike, everything seemed so different—like I was a part of the nature around me. We started to pick up speed, and the warm wind whipped around us as we jetted around the deep curves of the road. It was amazing, so much so that I was disappointed when the sun started to set, and we headed back to my apartment. I wasn't ready for my time with him to end. It seemed I always felt like that when I was with him, and I had a strong suspicion that wasn't going to change any time soon.

HAWK

*A*fter weeks of busting our asses, the new strip club was up and running. Just as we'd hoped, opening night was a huge success. Hell, the place was busting at the seams with all kinds of people. Men and women were all gathered around the stage, drinking and carrying on as they watched our girls put on a show. The guys and I were feeling pretty good about the turnout as we sat in the back, drinking a few beers and enjoying the benefits of all our hard work. I was about to take another shot of tequila when Misty, one of the strippers, came over to the table. She wasn't wearing much, just a miniskirt that barely covered her ass and a halter top that was less of a top and more of a sheer bra, revealing every inch her cleavage. All eyes were on her as she gave me a sexy smile and purred, "Can I get you boys anything?"

"Another round of shots would be good. Just put it on the club's tab."

"Sure thing."

She gave me a wink, then turned and sauntered over

to the bar. Rafe nudged with his elbow and snickered. "Looks like our boy is gonna get laid tonight."

"Maybe so, but not by the likes of her."

"Why the hell not?" He huffed. "That chick is smoking hot."

"Not interested."

"What the fuck is wrong with you, brother? I'd let her ride my dick any time."

"Some chick has her hooks in our boy," Axel poked.

"Seriously?" Rafe looked over to me like I had three heads. "How the fuck did that happen?"

Before I had a chance to respond, Misty strolled back over and placed our shots on the table, then glanced at me with another smile. "Here you go, boys. Can I get you anything else?"

"That should do it."

"You sure?" She leaned closer, her tits just inches from my face as she whispered, "One of the rooms in the back just opened up. I'd be happy to give you a private lap-dance or anything else you might want."

A few weeks ago, I wouldn't have thought twice about taking her up on that offer. Hell, I'd have given her the pounding of a lifetime, but at the moment, I couldn't have been less interested—maybe it was the fact that I just wanted to enjoy some time with my brothers or maybe it was Delilah. Whatever the reason, I reached over and patted Rafe on the shoulder. "I'm good, but my brother is up for a go."

"Oh, really?" She turned her flirtatious smile towards him. "I'd be down for that."

Rafe grabbed a shot from the table, and once he tossed it back, he stood up and said, "I'm ready when you are."

He followed Misty towards the back, and when they disappeared into one of the rooms, I took another shot. As I lowered the empty glass to the table, Axel leaned over to me and asked, "So, what's up with you and Danny's sister? Y'all a thing now or what?"

"Working on it."

"Really." He studied me for a moment, then leaned back in his chair with a knowing smirk. "I gotta say, I didn't see that one coming."

"You're not the only one."

"You think she'll be able to get past everything that went down with Danny?"

"It might take some time, but yeah, she'll get past it."

"Hope you're right." He motioned over to one of the waitresses and ordered a round of beers. "Otherwise, this thing between you two ended before it even got started."

His words packed a hell of punch, but I knew he was right. The club was my life, and if Delilah continued to hold on to her grudge, no matter how valid, things with us would never work. I could tell her a million times over that my brothers were good guys, but it wouldn't change a damn thing. She needed to see it for herself. There was just one catch—*Danny*. He wasn't a quick healer like Rafe. He was still on the mend, and Viper still hadn't made the call on what we were going to do with him. As long as he remained at the club, especially with a fucking gunshot wound, there was no way I could bring her to the clubhouse, so I'd have to figure out another way for her to spend some time with the guys. That thought had me turning to Axel and Menace. "Hey, what do you two got going on tomorrow?"

"Nothing much that I can think of. Why?"

"I got something I need you to do."

I explained the plan to them, and just as I'd expected, they both were more than willing to help me out. After one last drink, I said my goodbyes and headed out. A half hour later, I was sitting outside Delilah's apartment. I hadn't intended on stopping by, but I found myself there just the same. I glanced up at her place and all the lights were out. I wasn't surprised. It was almost midnight, and she had work early the next morning. As much as I wanted to crawl into bed next to her, I decided against it, thinking she could use the rest. I was just about to leave when a black truck caught my attention across the street. If it hadn't been for the faint glow of a burning cigarette, I would've never noticed the guy sitting inside. It was too dark to see his face, but there was something about him that gave me an uneasy feeling. I got off my bike and started walking over to him, but as I got closer, he eased out of the parking space and skirted off down the street. Thinking Menace might be able to check him out, I tried to get a look at the guy's license plate, but it was too dark to make it out.

A short time later, I finally convinced myself that I was making something out of nothing and got back on my bike. I took one last look up at Delilah's apartment, then headed home for the night. When I woke up the next morning, I got dressed and went over to the clubhouse to meet up with Axel and Menace. When I pulled through the gate, I found them both waiting at the front door with Viper. Axel walked over to me and said, "We're ready when you are."

"Prez coming along too?"

"Yeah, I filled him in on what we were doing, and he

wanted to join in. Widow, too. He's going to meet us there."

"Appreciate that."

"No problem, brother. Glad to do it."

With that, he and the others got on their bikes and followed me over to the nursing home. When we arrived, Widow was waiting for us in the parking lot. We parked next to him, then headed inside. I was checking in at the front desk when I spotted Delilah walking towards us with a concerned look across her face "Hey, what's going on?"

"If it's all right, the guys and I thought we'd visit with Mr. McClanahan for a bit."

"Really?" She looked over at my brothers and smiled. "That's sweet of you to think of him. I'm sure he would've enjoyed seeing you, but he's not doing very well today."

"Oh? What's going on?"

"We're not sure. His blood pressure has been up and down all morning, and he's a bit disorientated." I could hear the worry in her voice as she added, "I'm not sure he'd be up for a visit. It might be too much for him."

"I don't know," the nurse behind the desk interrupted. "I think he might enjoy some company."

"Are you sure?"

"Yeah, I think it'll be good for him." The nurse handed Delilah a clipboard. "Go with them and monitor his vitals. As long as they're good, the guys are welcome to sit with him."

"Okay." Delilah looked back over to us as she said, "Come on. I'll show you to his room."

We all followed Delilah down to McClanahan's room, and when we walked in, he was lying in the bed with his eyes closed. Delilah walked over to the edge of the bed and placed her hand on his arm, giving him a gentle shake as she leaned over him and whispered, "Mr. McClanahan, you have some visitors."

"Hmm," McClanahan groaned. "What visitors?"

"You remember Hawk, don't you?" With squinted eyes, he looked over at me, and his face lit up when he noticed the brothers behind me. "They wanted to chat with you for a bit, if you're up for it."

He eased up on the bed and smiled. "Of course, I'm up for it. Glad to see you again, Hawk. Good of you to come by."

"Delilah mentioned you were having a bad morning. You doing okay?"

"Yeah, I'm fine." He placed his hand on his chest. "The old ticker is trying to play out on me, but I'm not ready to call it quits just yet."

"Good to hear that." I motioned my hand over to Viper. "I'm not sure if you've met my president. This is Viper. Also brought along my VP, Axel. And next to him is Menace and Widow."

"Good of you boys to come down like this." McClanahan turned his attention to Viper as he said, "Heard good things about you, son. Sounds like you run a steady ship over there at the Ruthless Sinners."

"I do my best." A smile crept over my president's face as he told him, "I heard the same thing about you. The Ravens are a good group of men."

"They are." Sadness filled his eyes as McClanahan muttered, "Miss those boys. Wish I could see them more."

"Maybe we could do something about that."

"Maybe." He thought for a moment, then said, "You

boys ever ridden the Tail of the Dragon up near the Carolina border?"

The Tail of the Dragon had always been popular with bikers. They came from all over the world to ride the eleven mile stretch down US 129. The desolate, wooded roadside isn't for the faint of heart. The highway is filled with twists and turns that any biker would get a thrill out of riding, but with all the animal life and possible downed trees, it can make it dangerous to travel on a motorcycle. A smile crossed Widow's face as he nodded. "Hell, yeah. Ridden it many times. One of my favorite places to ride."

I glanced over at Delilah, and she was all smiles as she sat back and listened in on our conversation. Every now and then, she'd take a moment to check McClanahan's heart monitor, but I could tell from her expression that we had nothing to worry about. He was hanging in there just fine and clearly enjoying himself. McClanahan shook his head as he said, "I remember the first time I took my Clarice out on that road. Thought she'd squeeze the life right out of me."

"I bet. It's definitely not a road for the squeamish," I replied. "Natchez Trace is also a good one."

"Hell, yeah, it is. Nothing better in this world than being out on the open road with the brothers. I wouldn't trade those days for anything." McClanahan glanced up at the ceiling as he tried to get a grip on his emotions. "You boys still ruling the roost downtown?"

"Doing what we can," Viper answered. "It seems like it's getting harder and harder these days."

"With a good, strong leader like you, those boys of yours can handle anything."

We continued to talk, and in what seemed like no time,

two hours had passed. McClanahan was starting to grow tired, so Delilah stood up and said, "I hate to cut things short, but I think it's time for our friend here to get some much-needed rest."

"No need to rush off. I'm fine," he argued.

"As much as we've enjoyed it, we best get going," I interjected. "Besides, we wouldn't want to upset the boss lady."

"Yeah," McClanahan looked over to Delilah and smiled. "She can be a real stickler when she has to be."

I glanced over at Delilah. "I know that all too well."

"Let's move it, boys," Delilah ordered with a smirk.

We each said our goodbyes to McClanahan, and as we started out the door, Delilah called out to us. "Hey! Wait a second."

Viper turned to her and asked, "Yeah?"

"I just wanted to thank you for coming." There was no missing the sincerity of her voice as she said, "It meant a lot to Mr. McClanahan, and it really meant a lot to me."

"Glad to do it."

"Well, thanks again, and I hope you guys can make it back sometime."

"Definitely." Viper gave her a quick wink. "Good to see ya, Delilah."

When he turned to walk away, the others followed, giving me a moment alone with Delilah. I leaned forward and kissed her, then said, "I better get going, but I'll see you later tonight."

"Okay." As I turned to walk away, she called out, "Be careful."

"Always."

When I reached the others, they were already on their

bikes and ready to go. I slipped on my helmet, and just as I was about to start up the engine, Viper looked over to me and said, "I gotta admit, I had my concerns about your girl being able to keep her mouth shut with everything that went down with her brother, but she's done all right. Looks like you might've been right about her after all."

Without giving me a chance to respond, he pulled out of his parking spot and started towards the exit. The rest of us quickly followed suit, and as we drove back to the clubhouse, I was feeling pretty fucking good about things. Delilah seemed pleased by our visit, and Viper was starting to come around where she was concerned. I couldn't blame him for having his doubts. Hell, I had plenty of my own, but time and time again, she'd not only proven herself to me but to everyone around her.

When we got back to the clubhouse, Viper called all the brothers in for church. It had been several days since we'd met, and he wanted to fill us in on some new developments. As soon as we were gathered in the conference room, Viper stood and said, "Before we get started, I want to commend you on all your hard work getting the new club up and going. I think you'll each agree that last night was a big success."

"Absolutely," Axel replied. "Only one thing would've made it better."

"I'm about to get to that." Viper's smile faded as he said, "You all know about our issues with our last shipment and the fallout that came after. That being said, it's time for us to nail down a new dealer, one that we can trust, with the means to handle the demands of two clubs. Axel and I have been looking into it, and we think we might've found someone."

"You feel good about them?"

"It's hard to say," Viper answered. "In my gut, I think he's our man, but after the way things played out with Danny, I think it would be in our best interest to do a little more digging into this guy. We need to know everything there is about him before we make a move." Viper turned to Menace and said, "I'll get you everything we have on him, and you see if he has any skeletons in his closet that we should know about."

"You got it."

"What about Miller and Danny?" Rafe asked. "How we handling all that?"

"Miller has been dealt with—Billy had his boys take Miller's car and set it up to look like the guy bolted with both the cash and the drugs, taking any speculation that we were involved off the table." Viper let out a deep breath, then said, "Danny, on the other hand, is a different story altogether. While he wasn't the one behind the counterfeit drugs, he did try to skip out on us, and he shot Rafe ... twice."

"Ah, I'm all right, Prez. Besides, the kid was scared shitless." Rafe could've easily held a grudge against Danny, but it was in his nature to just let things go, so I wasn't surprised when Rafe said, "He knew what was coming, and if I was in his shoes, I probably would've done the same fucking thing."

"He shot you—a brother of the Ruthless Sinners. You don't do that shit and get away with it," Viper argued.

"He didn't." Rafe nodded his head to his left. "Shotgun made sure of that."

"You saying we should just let this kid walk?"

"I don't see why we wouldn't." Rafe shrugged. "I know

he panicked and all that, and didn't come forward to set things right, but he wasn't the one who tried to pull one over on us. And don't forget ... he took a bullet for you."

"Rafe's got a point," Axel agreed. "You both do. He fucked up when he shot Rafe, but he's come a long way in making up for it."

"That he did." Knowing how much it would mean to Delilah that her brother would soon be free, relief washed over me when Viper said, "We'll let him walk. Who knows? Maybe having him around will come in handy someday."

"You never know. It just might."

"The day's wasting away, boys." Viper stood as he said, "Get out there and make the best of it."

We all got up from the table and slowly dispersed. I stopped and had a few words with Axel and Viper, thanking them again for going over to the nursing home with me to see McClanahan. As soon as we were done talking, I headed over to Delilah's place. I was just about to enter the apartment complex when I noticed the black truck from the night before whipping around the corner. Once again, he was going too fast for me grab the fuckin' license plate. Having no choice, I let it go and continued upstairs to her place. I'd barely knocked when she opened the door and smiled. Her scrubs from earlier had been replaced with a pair of running shorts and a long-sleeved, tie-dyed t-shirt. Her hair was down, and she was wearing just a hint of makeup, but she didn't need it. Delilah was a natural beauty who looked amazing with little effort. "Hey... come on in. Dinner's almost ready."

She closed the door, then rushed back into the

kitchen. "What are we having?" I asked as I stepped inside her apartment.

"Tenderloin and veggies." As she checked the potatoes, she looked over to me and said, "You were pretty clever today."

"Really? How so?"

"Bringing the guys to the nursing home like you did." She gave me one of her little smirks. "I know you had ulterior motives."

"Oh? And what was that?"

"You bringing them over to see Mr. McClanahan wasn't just for him. It was for me too." Her eyes narrowed as she stared at me and said, "You were hoping I'd get to see a different side of them."

"Um-hmm." I eased over to her and wrapped my arms around her waist, pulling her close. "And did it work?"

"Yeah, pretty much." A smile crept across her beautiful face as she said, "I gotta admit, I was kind of surprised. They were all really great with him, and it meant a lot to Mr. McClanahan. He wouldn't stop talking about it. As a matter of fact, everyone in the nursing home was going on about you guys."

"I'm glad to hear that, but I want you to know ... I would've gone back to see McClanahan regardless of what happened with us, and sooner or later, the guys would've ended up coming along too." I kissed her lightly on the neck. "I just sped up the process a bit."

"I know." Her expression grew soft as she tucked a loose strand of hair behind her ear. "That's one of the things I like about you."

"One of the things?" I took a step back and looked down at her. "So, there's more?"

"Yeah, there's plenty more." Her blue eyes never left mine as she said, "I like that you're a little self-absorbed, and yet so very thoughtful of others. I like that you're confident when you're right, but you'll admit when you're wrong. I also like the fact that you're this rough and tough biker, but at the same time, you can be the most gentle man I've ever met."

Damn. I'd never had anyone sum me up quite like that before. We'd only known each other for a couple of weeks, but she nailed it. Delilah knew me even better than I knew myself, making me realize, now more than ever, that I'd found the one. Delilah was like no woman I'd ever met. She was it for me. No doubt about it. Consumed with emotion, I leaned down and pressed my lips to hers, kissing her long and hard, showing her exactly how much she meant to me. The kiss led us into the bedroom, and I knew the second I started to remove her clothes, dinner was going to be late—very late.

DELILAH

Things with Zander were going well—*even better than I'd ever imagined*. I never dreamed that I'd fall in love with him and could be so utterly happy, especially given all the secrets and being kept in the dark about what was going on with Danny's situation. Even though he hadn't actually said the words, I had a feeling that things were going to be okay with my brother. Zander had never given me any indication otherwise, so I was doing my best to hold on to the hope that someday soon I'd be seeing him again. Besides, Zander was a good man, and he was close to proving that his brothers were too. There was just one thing that gave me doubts—the person in the black truck who had been stalking me for the last week or so.

I assumed it was one of Zander's brothers, but he was different than the others. When I'd walk by in the mornings, his brothers would at least nod or smile, giving me some kind of acknowledgement. I knew why they were there. I knew they were watching me in case I opened my mouth and went to the police about what had happened with Danny, but there was something about them being there that I found oddly comforting. The same didn't hold true for the new guy. There was something about him that gave me the creeps. He just sat there behind his dark tented windows, staring at me as I walked by—day and night. And honestly, I didn't even understand why he was there—especially since the circumstances had changed. Zander spent most nights at my place, or I at his. I'd given the Sinner's no reason to think that I would go against my word, so it didn't make sense that they'd suddenly chosen to increase their surveillance.

As I started down the steps and towards the parking lot, I decided not to make a big deal of the fact that he was sitting there, yet again. Instead, I looked over to the guy sitting behind the steering wheel, smoking his stupid cigarette, and gave him a big wave. He did nothing—just sat there completely motionless. Acting complete unbothered by the fact that he didn't return the gesture, I smiled and continued towards my car. I kept smiling as I got in and drove away. I thought I'd handled the situation very well, until the asshole started to follow me to my mother's house. That's was something the other brothers hadn't done, and I'd had enough. There was absolutely no reason for him to follow me there, so I pressed my foot against the accelerator and started zipping through traffic, doing my best to lose him. Even with my best efforts, he managed to stay close behind, but then I got lucky. Just was I was coming up on a traffic light, a massive dump truck pulled in front of him, forcing him to stop. I quickly turned down a busy street, and after making several more turns, I finally lost him and continued on to Mom's house.

When I walked in, I found her sitting at the kitchen table, and even though it was well into the afternoon, she was still in her pajamas, drinking a cup of coffee. "Good morning."

"Hi, sweetheart." She looked up and smiled. "I was hoping you would stop by."

"I promised I would." After I made myself a glass of tea, I went over and sat down next to her. "I would've come sooner, but I've been swamped at work."

"Oh." She looked over me with knowing eyes as she said, "I thought you might've met someone."

"What makes you say that?"

"I don't know. You just seem different... *happier*. I was hoping you might've found yourself a young man to date."

"Well, it just so happens that I have been seeing someone." I couldn't go into all the details of who Zander was or how we'd actually met, so I told her, "He's not like any of the guys I've gone out with before, but I'm starting to think that might be a good thing."

"Will I get to meet this new guy of yours?"

"Maybe. Let's see how things go first."

"Okay. Whatever you think. Just know that if you like this boy, I will, too." She let out a sigh as she said, "Maybe someday Danny will meet someone special, too. That's if he's even okay. I'm really having my doubts that he is."

"I don't know." I didn't want to give her false hope, but it was so hard to see her so upset. "I think we'll be hearing something from him soon."

"Really? What makes you think so?"

"I can't say for sure. Just a gut feeling, I guess."

"I'd like to think you're right, but this has gone on too long." I could hear the determination in her voice and panic started to build in the pit of my stomach when she said, "It's time to find out what's going on with him, Delilah. If the roles were reversed and it was you who'd been missing for weeks, I would've already contacted the police. Danny would've insisted on it."

As much as I hated to do it, I had to think of some way to put her off, even if it was just for a little longer, so I said, "How about this? I have a friend that works at the police station. Why don't I go down there and talk to him? See what he thinks we should do."

"That would be great." She stood up, and as she started towards her bedroom, she said, "Let me get changed, and I'll go with you."

"Mom, wait!" I stood up and walked over to her. "Let me do this on my own. He'll be much more open to talk if it's just me."

Disappointment crossed her face as she said, "Oh, okay. I understand."

"I'll let you know what he says." I gave her a quick hug. "I love you, Mom."

"I love you, too, sweetheart."

"I'll give you a call soon."

"Okay."

When I got out to my car, I pulled out my phone and sent Zander a text, letting him know that we needed to talk and to call me back. As soon as I was done, I pulled out of my mother's driveway and started downtown. I'd promised Krissy that I would meet her for dinner, and we'd do a little shopping after. I was hoping to talk to Zander about my mother, but I still hadn't heard from him when I got to the restaurant. I tried to push it to the back of my mind as I parked my car and walked inside to find Krissy. It was a small Italian place with a great little outdoor sitting area, which was where I found Krissy waiting for me. I went over, and the second I sat down, she gave me a look. My dear, sweet, annoyingly perceptive friend could always tell when something was bothering me, so I wasn't surprised when she asked, "What's wrong?"

"It's nothing really." The weight started to lift off my shoulders as I continued, "It's just Danny. He's gone off the rails again."

"What do you mean?"

"It's hard to explain. He just hasn't been around in a while, and Mom's freaking out about it." I shook my head. "I tried to explain to her that he'll show up eventually, but she isn't listening. She wants to go to the police about it."

"Maybe you should, especially if it's been several days."

"Well, that's just it." I was walking on thin ice as I told her, "I can't."

"Why not?"

"Because of who he's mixed up with. I'm afraid that getting the police involved will only make things worse."

"Oh. Well, that sheds a different light on things." She thought for a moment, then asked, "Is there someone you could ask about him? Find out if he's okay or not?"

"Yeah ... I can push a little harder and see what I can find out."

"That might not be a bad idea. You could always explain the situation with your mother wanting to call the police and see if that makes a difference."

"You're right. That actually might help."

"Do you want to skip dinner and go tend to Danny? I understand if you do."

"Are you sure you don't mind?"

"Of course not," she assured me. "We can meet up anytime."

"Okay ... Thanks for understanding." I grabbed my purse and stood up. "I'll give you a call later."

"Good luck, girl, and let me know if I can do anything."

"I will."

I headed out to my car, and once I was inside, I tried calling Zander for a second time. Again, no answer. I felt like I was running out of time, so I started the car and tried to remember my way to the clubhouse. It had been a while since that morning when Zander had taken me back to Danny's place, but I didn't think I would have any trouble finding my way there. Unfortunately, I was wrong. So many of the roads looked familiar, but none of them were the ones that led to the clubhouse.

After an hour of going in circles, I was getting frustrated and just about to stop and ask for directions when a tall fence caught my attention. As I got closer to the building, I spotted the large gated entrance, and I knew I'd finally found it. I pulled up to the man standing guard and asked, "Is this the Ruthless Sinners' clubhouse?"

"Who's asking?"

"I'm Delilah Davenport. I'm looking for Zander ... I mean Hawk."

"Hold on a minute." He stepped away from my car and pulled out his phone. After several long moments, he came back over to me. "Pull up to the front. Stay there and wait. He'll be out as soon as he can."

"Okay, thanks."

I did as I was told and pulled my car up to the front of the building. Once I was parked, I turned off the engine.

As I sat there waiting, I looked around the parking lot and the tall fence that surrounded it, and it wasn't long before all those forgotten feelings of doubt and anxiousness I'd had the last time I was there came rushing back. I found myself wanting to barge inside and demand to see my brother, to finally see for myself what was really going on with him, but I didn't move, fearing I'd only end up locked away again. I had worked myself up into a nervous fit when Zander finally stepped out the front door and walked over to my car. His brows were furrowed in confusion as he opened the door and asked, "What are you doing here, Delilah?"

"I have to talk to you about Danny." When I saw a spark of annoyance flash through his eyes, I continued, "Before you get upset with me, I want you to hear me out. There are things you need to know."

"Such as?"

"My mother is worried about him. She's been trying to find him since the night you brought him here, and she's starting to freak out." I got out of my car and stood next to him. "I've been trying to convince her that she just needs to just give it some time, but she isn't listening. She wants to go to the police."

"No need for that."

"I know. I've been trying to tell her that, but I can only put her off for so long, Zander," I argued. "She's his *mother*, and she's concerned. I can only imagine how freaked out she'd be if she actually knew the truth about what was going on."

"You're not listening to me, Delilah. I'm telling you, there's no need for her to go to the cops. Danny's good."

"I am listening, Zander, but you've been saying the

same thing for the past few weeks. As far as I can tell, nothing's changed." Since we were on the topic of Danny, I decided it was a good time to mention the recent upgrade in surveillance. "And while we're at it, I hope you know I've really been trying with all this. Even though I've been very tempted, I haven't said anything I wasn't supposed to. I've held up my end of the bargain and kept my mouth shut."

"I know. You've done good, Delilah."

"Really, 'cause it sure doesn't seem that way."

"Not sure what you're talking about," he argued.

"I'm talking about y'all watching me every second of every day." My mind was racing with worry, making it difficult to think straight. I knew I was rambling and not giving him much chance to respond, but I couldn't seem to help myself. "I thought you and your brothers would ease up once I proved myself, but I guess that's not going to happen."

"Delilah, I honestly don't know what you're talking about." A few of the guys stepped out of the clubhouse, momentarily drawing his attention away from me. They each spoke but continued on their way. "You know we've been keeping an eye on you. There's no reason for me to deny that, but you haven't given us any reason to think we'd need to keep watching you every second."

"Then, I don't get it. What's with the creeper in the black truck?" I snapped back. "Why is he suddenly there all the time, watching—"

Before I could finish my thought, the door opened once again. Two other bikers came barreling out, and following close behind them was my brother. My mind immediately went blank. I couldn't believe my eyes. He was smiling like his usual happy-go-lucky self without a care in the world, and he was cutting up with Zander's brothers like they were old buddies of his. He looked nothing like he did the last time I'd seen him. Instead of blood-soaked clothes, he was wearing a clean t-shirt with jeans, the bruises and swelling had faded, and other than the sling and a slight limp, he looked like himself. I couldn't make sense of it. If I didn't know better, I would've thought that Danny was one of them—a brother of the Ruthless Sinners. They were all so caught up in their conversation that he didn't even notice me.

"Danny?"

He stopped dead in his tracks as he turned to me. "Delilah? What are you doing here?"

"I came here to see about you. What the hell is going on? I thought ..." I turned to Zander and said, "I don't understand what's happening here."

"No need to get all worked up, Dee." Danny fussed. "I'm good. Me and the brothers worked things out. Things are gonna be okay. You don't have to worry anymore."

"So ... what? After everything that happened, you're suddenly all good with them?"

"Yeah, actually, I am."

I couldn't believe my ears. My brother had clearly lost his ever-loving mind. Trying to bring him to his senses, I motioned my hand to his sling as I asked, "And what about your arm? Did they do this to you too?"

"No."

"No? Then, what happened?"

"Well ... about that. I was shot. It wasn't a big deal, though," he answered casually. "Bullet went straight through, and I'm fine."

"You were shot?" I gasped. "When the hell did that happen?"

Zander cut his eyes over to Danny, and the color quickly drained from his face when he realized he'd said too much. "I can't get into all that, but look ... I'm fine, Dee. There's no reason to make a big deal of this."

"And why would I make a big deal of it? I'm just finding out that my brother was not only tortured—but shot. That's not a big deal at all ... I would be crazy to make a big deal out of that!" Feeling utterly betrayed, I turned to look at Zander. "I can't believe you kept this from me. All the times I asked you about him, and never once did you mention that he'd been hurt! After everything, how could you just lie to me like this?"

"I didn't lie to you, Delilah."

"Well, you certainly didn't tell me the truth. You were too busy protecting your brothers and your precious club." I threw my hands up and said, "You know what? Forget it. I'm done. I'm done with *all of it*. I didn't sign up for this—any of it. You can have your club, you can even have my brother, but you can't have me. *Not like this*."

When I started to get back into my car, Zander called out to me, "Delilah, Wait."

Seeing the anguish in his eyes tore at me, but I was too hurt to stand there and listen to his excuses. I'd trusted him, and even though Danny had obviously forgiven them for everything they'd done, I just couldn't do it. I got in my car, and before I closed the door, I looked at Zander and said, "This is just too much. I can't do it."

Saying those words to him killed me. I loved Zander. I didn't want things to end, but I couldn't make the same mistakes my mother had made. I needed to know that I could trust the man I loved, and I clearly couldn't trust Zander—at least not in the way I needed to. I fought back the tears as I slammed my door and started my car. Without looking back at either Zander or Danny, I pulled out of the parking lot and sped through the gate. I tried to keep it together as long as I could, but as soon as I was out on the main road, the damn broke and tears started to stream down my face. I wanted to think I'd done the right thing by walking away, but the throbbing ache in my chest made me wonder if I'd made a terrible mistake. That doubt weighed heavily on me as I pulled up to my apartment, got out of my car, and started upstairs.

As soon as I stepped inside, I knew something didn't feel right. I figured it was just my mind playing tricks on me, so I ignored the voice in my head that told me something was wrong. I tossed my keys and purse on the counter like I always did, then, without turning on the lights, I headed towards my room. I hadn't gotten far when I heard a familiar voice call out to me, "Well ... hello, *Delilah.*"

HAWK

I stood there under a blanket of darkness, feeling completely powerless as I watched the taillights of her car disappear into the night. I wanted to call out to her, demand her to stay, but I couldn't. Deep down, I knew she was doing the right thing by leaving. That didn't mean it didn't hurt like hell to watch her go. Fuck, it had taken me a lifetime to find Delilah, and it gutted me to think I'd actually lost her. My hands were tied. If I'd told her what had happened with Danny, she would've had questions—questions I couldn't begin to answer. I'd hoped the fact that he was set free would be enough to appease her, but I should've known that wouldn't have been the case. I was still standing there, staring off into the darkness, when Danny stepped over to me.

"What was that all about?" His eyes narrowed as he stood there studying me. "You got something going on with my sister?"

"You could say that."

"Damn, I didn't see that one coming," he scoffed.

"I don't think anyone did."

"You're a brave man to get involved with my sister." He snickered as he said, "Dee is a hard-ass, man. Doesn't let anything slide by."

"I'm aware."

"No offense, man, but"—he ran his hand through his long shaggy hair—"After everything that happen, I'm surprised she didn't tell you to fuck off."

"You're not the only one."

"I'm not one to judge. Fuck, I've never had any kind of relationship that was worth a damn, but Dee's got a good head on her shoulders. She thinks things through ... Something I've never been very good at. So, if she gave you a chance, there had to be reason." Danny looked over to me as he continued, "I'm guessing she saw some good in you; otherwise, she wouldn't have given ya a second thought."

"If that's the case, then she was wrong."

"I don't know, man. I got no idea what kind of fella you really are. Still trying to figure that shit all out. I do know that the lifestyle you got going on here is a lot different than what she's used to. Hell, it's a lot different than what I'm used to, but that's not a bad thing. I've seen how you guys interact with one another. It's like you're more than just a club or whatever. You stick together and have each other's back. Even the way you handled me. You did what you had to do to protect the club. You gotta respect that."

"Not sure she saw it that way."

"So, what?" His eyes narrowed as he asked, "You're just gonna give up on her?"

"I can't force Delilah to see things my way, Danny."

"No, but you can do your best to make her understand." Sounding completely sincere, he offered, "You know, I could go talk to her. Explain things the way I see 'em and maybe set things right."

"I don't think that's a good idea."

Once Viper had given the word that Danny would be released, he gave him limited range of the clubhouse, allowing him time to finish healing from his gunshot wound instead of just forcing him out the door. It was a decision none of us expected. I had a feeling that Viper saw something in Danny and wanted the opportunity to see if his instincts about him were right. While I had my doubts at first, I had to admit that he wasn't at all like I'd expected. Similar to his sister, he had a good head on his shoulders and had completely owned up to his mistakes. Hell, he didn't even hold a grudge against Shotgun, understanding that he was doing his part to protect the brothers. As I stood there talking to him, I could see him as being a good addition to the club, but I had my doubts that his sister would feel the same. I looked at Danny and said, "I think I need to give her some time."

"Maybe so." Danny glanced behind him, watching the guys as they sat around the fire drinking a cold one. "How about a couple of beers? Might help take your mind off things for a bit."

"Doubt it, but you go ahead. I'll catch up with you guys later."

"You got it, man." He turned to leave, but quickly

stopped and looked back at me. "Hey, I was meaning to ask you ... Have the guys been watching Delilah?"

"Yeah, we had to be sure she wouldn't talk about you and everything that happened."

"I get it. Did Delilah know y'all were watching her?"

"We didn't keep that a secret." I sighed. "Figured it would help motivate her to keep her mouth shut."

"She didn't talk, did she?"

"Not a word."

"Didn't think she would. Delilah isn't one to go back on her word." Apprehension crossed his face as he said, "So, this creeper she was talking about ... He something I need to be concerned about?"

"Honestly, I'm not sure." I'd seen the guy and hadn't forgotten the uneasy feeling I got after I noticed him parked outside her apartment. At the time, I hadn't known for certain if he was there for her, but now that I did, it made my blood run cold to think he might do something to hurt her. I needed to know for sure that he had no connection to the club, so I told Danny, "I'll talk to Viper and see if he knows anything about it."

"Okay, sounds good," he replied, sounding relieved. "If you don't mind, let me know what he says."

"Will do."

When Danny turned to join the others, I went inside the clubhouse to find Viper. He and Menace had been going over the intel Menace had collected on Flint, the new dealer we were looking into. With the new club open and doing so well, we wanted to get product moving before our customers went looking somewhere else. Even though Viper was eager to get our first order placed, he wasn't going to make a move until he was certain that we'd found the right guy. When I walked into his office, they were both gathered around his desk, going over all the files. "How's our guy looking?"

"Pretty good, actually," Viper answered. "I'm not seeing any red flags yet, so I'd say that's a good sign."

"That's a very good sign. So, now what?"

"I'm thinking we'll place a small order and just see how it plays out. If the product is as good as they say it is, then we'll be set."

"That's great to hear. It'll be good to finally get the ball moving on this. Just let me know if you need me to do anything."

"You know I will." He lowered the papers onto his desk, giving me his full attention. "You got something on your mind?"

"Yeah, I need to ask you about something."

Menace stood up, and as he started out of the room, he said, "I'll give you two a minute."

Once he'd closed the door, Viper looked up at me and asked, "What's going on?"

"It's about Delilah."

"Yeah?"

"Do you know anything about a guy who's been watching her? He drives a black truck ... been sitting outside her place and hangin' around."

A puzzled expression crossed his face, and I knew right then he didn't have a clue. "I don't know anything about it. Hell, I put you in charge of watching her, so if there's anyone who'd know about a new guy, it'd be you."

"Damn, I was afraid you were going to say that."

"So, she's got some guy watching her. You got any idea why?"

"I wish I did."

"How long has it been going on?"

"Apparently, he's been at it a while—a week or more." I let out a deep breath. "She thought it was one of the brothers, so she didn't mention anything about it until she came by here tonight."

"When was this?"

"Hasn't been long since she left. Twenty minutes or so. She was pretty upset when she got here." I thought back to the moment she stepped out of her car. I was glad that she'd come, but I didn't get a chance to tell her. Hell, I didn't get a chance to tell her much of anything. "She was freaking out over her mother wanting to go to the cops about Danny."

"You set her straight about him."

"I was about to, but Danny beat me to it. He came outside when we were talking. Needless to say, she was pretty torn up that I hadn't told her he'd been shot. Things went south from there."

"She took it pretty hard, huh?"

"Yeah. She left on a pretty sour note," I grumbled under my breath. "I didn't expect it would go well. Her brother means a lot to her. For that matter, her whole family does. There's nothing she wouldn't do for them."

"That's a good thing. It's important to have those ties to family. Those binds will see you through some hard times, and Delilah having them says a lot about her." He ran his hand over his thick beard as he mulled things over for a moment. "You think she'll come around?"

"Hard to say. She had her mind pretty set when she left

here." My chest tightened at the thought of actually losing her. I never imagined it would happen, not to me, but I'd fallen in love with her. I knew she deserved more than I could ever give her, but I didn't have it in me to just let her walk away—not without a fight. "But I'm not giving up on her. I can't."

"You really got something for this girl, don't ya?"

I nodded. "She's everything I never knew I wanted. I'm just afraid I've fucked it all up and lost her."

"I doubt that."

"I don't know, brother. When she sets her mind to something, it's hard to change it."

"Same with most women." Viper chuckled. "Just give it some time. She'll come around. For now, we need to be figuring out who's staking out her place. Find out what the hell he's up to."

"I couldn't agree more."

"You think he's there now?"

"Can't say for sure." I shook my head and scoffed. "I'd call her to ask, but something tells me she wouldn't answer."

"Well then, you best get over and see for yourself," Viper suggested. "Try and get this guy's license plate number or something. Anything we can use to find out who he is and why he's got a sudden interest in Delilah."

"I'll head over there now."

"Take one of the guys with you. Just in case."

"Will do. Thanks, Prez."

I gave him a nod, then left his office. When I got outside, I went over to the bonfire to find Shotgun. I quickly explained the situation with Delilah to him, and minutes later, we were headed over to our bikes. I was just about to start up my engine when Danny rushed over. Seeming unsure of himself, he shoved one of his hands into his pocket as he asked, "Hey, you going to see about Delilah?"

"Yeah, that's the plan."

"You mind if I tag along? I'd sure feel better if I knew what was going on."

"If this guy happens to be around"—I glanced down at Danny's sling—"I'm not sure you'd be any help to us with that bum shoulder."

"Probably not."

"Then I'd say it's best you just hang out here, man." I appreciated the fact that Danny wanted to check on his sister, but it was too risky. If we ran into trouble, he'd cause more harm than good. "If something's up, I'll be sure to let you know."

"Okay, sounds good." As he stepped away, he gave us a slight wave and said, "You guys be careful."

I nodded, and moments later, Shotgun and I were on our way to Delilah's place. As much as I wanted to go up to her apartment and talk things out, I knew it wasn't a good idea—at least not yet. I needed to give her some time to sort things out on her own, but that didn't mean I was just going to roll over and play dead. I'd waited too damn long find a woman like her, and now that I had, I wasn't going to give her up without a fight. One way or another, I would make her see that we were right for one another. When we pulled up to her place, I scanned the parking lot for the truck, but saw no sign of it. In fact, Delilah's was one of the few cars in the entire lot. Shotgun looked over to me as he asked, "You seeing anything?"

"Nope. Looks like the motherfucker took the night off."

"Any chance he'd be in a different vehicle?"

"Fuck if I know." I glanced up at Delilah's apartment, and other than one small lamp by the window, all the lights were off. Assuming she'd already gone to bed, I told him, "I guess I'll try again later."

"You don't want to go up and check on her?"

"Yeah, but that's not a good idea."

"Trouble in paradise already?" While I cared a great deal for all my brothers, Shotgun and I had always been close. I'd even go so far as to say he was my best friend. He knew me better than anyone and wasn't afraid to call me on my shit, so I wasn't surprised when he decided to give me a hard time about my present situation with Delilah. "Hmm ... Figured it would take you a little longer than a few weeks to fuck things up."

"So, you thinking this thing is my fault?"

He cocked his eyebrow and smirked. "Am I wrong?"

"No," I scoffed.

"Didn't think so." He crossed his arms and gave me one of his looks. "So, what are you gonna do about?"

"I'm gonna get her back."

He gave me a nod of approval. "That's my boy."

"I want to give this guy some time to show up. Let's take a ride downtown and make the loop?" I suggested. "Once we're done, we can swing back here, and maybe we'll catch sight of this guy before we head home."

"Sounds like a plan."

He gave me a nod, then he followed as I pulled out of the parking lot. As we drove towards downtown, I thought back to my life before Delilah. Back then, I never would've dreamed of getting involved with just one woman. The thought just didn't interest me. I was all about getting in and getting out, never giving any chick the opportunity of getting too close. Maybe I was just keeping my guard up, protecting myself from disappointment, or maybe it was the simple fact that I'd never met the right woman. Whatever the case, everything changed the minute I saw the fire in Delilah's eyes. It was a feeling that I didn't expect, and I was suddenly torn between what I'd always known and what I found myself wanting. I tried to ignore those feelings she stirred in me, but with each moment I spent with her, they only grew stronger. The pull I felt towards her was palpable, making me want things I'd never wanted before, and the mere thought of her being in danger was fucking with my head.

As we got closer to her place, I was becoming more and more on edge. I needed answers, and I was determined to find them as we pulled up to her apartment. Unfortunately, there was still no sign of the asshole anywhere. My patience was running thin as I looked up at Delilah's place. Just like earlier, all the lights were off except the one small lamp by the window. I was sitting there, staring up at her window, when I got the strangest sensation that someone was watching me. I took a quick glance around, but saw no one. Sensing my unease, Shotgun turned to me and asked, "You all right?"

It was getting late, and while I wasn't ready to leave, I had no doubt that he was. "You can head on back. I'm gonna stay here for a while and make sure this guy doesn't show."

"If you're staying, *I'm staying.*"

I nodded, then settled back in my seat. I looked back

up at Delilah's apartment, and even though I wished I was lying in the bed next to her, I found some small comfort in knowing she was close. That feeling was quickly replaced with an all-consuming dread when I noticed a large shadowy figure—one much too large to be Delilah—walk past her window.

DELILAH

I felt a cold chill run down my spine the minute I heard him say my name. I didn't have to see his face to know it was my father who was waiting for me there in the dark. It had been years since I'd seen him. In fact, the last time I did was the day Mom packed up all our stuff and we left. He didn't even say goodbye as we pulled out of the driveway and set out to start our new life without him. After that, I never heard from him again. No visits. No calls. Not so much as a birthday card. It was like he'd vanished from the earth, and I figured that was how things would always be—until tonight. I had no idea why he'd come, but the fact that he was sitting there, hidden in the dark corner of my apartment, gave me an unsettled feeling. Actually, it was more than that. It was terrifying. I did my best to swallow my fear as I stepped into the living room. "Dad?"

"Well, it's good to know my girl still recognizes me after all these years," he replied with sarcasm. "I must say, you've grown into a beautiful young woman. You look just like your mother did at your age."

"What are you doing here?"

"I've come to see you." He never moved from his spot. He just sat there, staring at me all cool, calm, and collected in his black dress slacks and dark gray button down. It was hard to see his face in the dark, but the way he was acting, it was clear that he thought there was nothing unusual about the fact that he'd broken into my home. I wanted nothing more than to lash out at him and tell him exactly what I thought, but I simply couldn't find the words. Instead, I just stood there listening as he said, "It's been a while. I thought it was time for us to catch up."

"*A while* is a bit of an understatement, don't you think?" I sassed. "It's been what? Fourteen years or more since I've seen or heard from you."

"Let's not get distracted by the details. Besides, that's all behind us now. It's time to move forward," he answered casually. "I see you're doing well for yourself. Got a nice place here. I guess working at a nursing home pays better than I thought."

"How do you know where I work?"

"I know everything about you, Delilah." His eyes met mine in a cold, angry stare. "What kind of father would I be if I didn't?"

"You've been watching me ... The man in the black truck. That was you?"

"That was one of my associates."

"Of course, it was," I snapped. "Why don't we just skip all the BS, Dad, and just tell me why you're really here."

"I already told you. I'm here to catch up. To reunite with my children." There was something about his tone that made my skin crawl. I had no interest in catching up with him, much less being in the same dark room with him. "In case you were wondering, I've done quite well for myself too. I've got my own business. It's been very successful until recently."

"Oh? And why's that? Did you gamble away all your profits?"

"You'd be wise to watch your tone with me, Delilah. I'm not the same man I used to be," he barked with a threatening tone.

"*Clearly.*"

"You know, I spent years listening to your mother's shit. She was always bitching because she couldn't see the bigger picture. I had plans. I knew what I was doing. If she'd just been patient, she could've had a much better life. You all could have." Before I could respond, he continued, "But that's all in the past. It's time for us to focus on the future."

"And how do you plan on us doing that?"

"For starters, you could tell me what is going on with your brother."

"I'm not sure I know what you mean." I crossed my arms and tried to keep my voice steady. "As far as I know, Danny's good."

"You sure about that?"

"What do you mean?"

"Danny came up missing just under a month ago, only a few days after he'd made a big delivery. Shortly after, a second associate of mine came up missing as well." He leaned forward, and for the first time I caught a glimpse of his face. He hadn't aged much, just a few sparse gray hairs here and there, but there was an evil look his eyes like I'd never seen before. A menacing expression crossed his face as he said, "I think the two are somehow connected."

"Why would they be connected? Danny doesn't have any ties to your associates."

"That's where you're wrong." He shot her an indignant glare and announced, "Danny has been working for me for almost five years now."

"What?" My mind was racing, making it difficult to think. I knew I had all the pieces to the puzzle, but I was having a hard time putting it all together. I took a deep breath and tried to calm the storm of thoughts racing through my head. After several moments, I was still at a loss. The only job Danny had that I knew about was selling drugs, and I couldn't understand what that had to do with my father. "How could he be working for you? He hasn't even seen you in years."

"Like I said, I've established quite a business for myself. I wanted to share my success by making Danny a part of it. I'll admit, he wasn't aware that I was behind this venture when he was offered to start dealing, but he's done well. There's a chance he could take over the entire business one day."

I was completely appalled. Our father, a man who was supposed to raise us, guide us, and keep us out of harm's way, had led his own son down a very treacherous path. To make matters worse, he seemed so offhanded about it, like it wasn't a big deal that his son was dealing drugs for him. I just couldn't fathom it. I wanted desperately to believe I was wrong, that he was talking about something else, so I asked, "Are you saying this business of yours, the one you got Danny involved in, is *dealing drugs*?"

"I'm providing a service, Delilah. A very profitable service."

"Are you insane? I don't care how profitable it might be. Dealing drugs is not only illegal, it's dangerous!" I knew I was being hypocritical. Hawk and his brothers were dealing the very drugs my father had sold to them, but I didn't hold the same animosity towards them that I had for my father. My rage towards him continued to build as I shouted, "Danny could get killed or land himself in jail, and for what? So you can make a dime? You repulse me."

"Just like your mother—self-righteous and judgmental. Think you know everything when you know nothing at all," my father snarled. "You know, she's fucking the reason Danny was weak. She taught him nothing. Hell, the boy could barely rub two pennies together before I came along."

"So, you think you came along and saved the day? Taught your son how to be a man and live a good life?" I shook my head in disgust. "You did it. Well done. You turned your son into drug dealer. I'm sure you're so proud."

"I am proud. Danny has done well for himself. And you should be proud of him too."

"And what happens when he gets caught? Are you going to be proud when he ends up in jail?"

"That won't happen. Since he started working for me, Danny has smartened up and become more like me. He's learned how to keep his head down and stay clear of any trouble."

I crossed my arms as I spat, "If that's so, then why is he suddenly missing?"

"We both know he isn't missing. At least, not anymore." In a low, threatening tone, he growled, "He's with those friends of yours ... the Ruthless Sinners."

"What makes you think they're friends of mine?"

"I already told you, Delilah. I know everything there is to know about you. Where you went to college. Where you work. What you drive. Where you spend your days and nights, and who you spend them with. I gotta say, I thought you were smarter than to get involved with men like those. You want to call me out for doing something that's illegal. What about them? Running strip clubs. Selling drugs to every Tom, Dick, and Harry. They're no better than me, and yet you'll spread your legs for them. Give them anything they want, including your brother. What does that say about you and all your *judgements*?"

"You have no idea what you're talking about!" I yelled. "You don't know me, and you certainly don't know them."

"I know enough." He leaned back into the dark shadows as he grumbled curses under his breath. "I know they think they've pulled a fast one over on me, but I'm too smart for that."

"I have no idea what you're talking about."

"Of course, you don't. When it comes to them, you only see what you want to see." For weeks, I'd held a grudge against the Sinners for what they'd done to Danny, and to me, but the day they came to the nursing home to see Mr. McClanahan, I saw a different side of them. Like Zander, they had a good side to them—one that was gentle and kind—and that side made me want to defend them, especially when my father said, "You know ... I've seen you with *him*. That biker with the cocky fucking smirk on his face, putting on airs like he's someone important, but he's nothing. I've crushed bigger men with the bottom of my fucking shoe."

"He's a better man than you'll ever be."

"You're a fool."

"I stopped caring about what you think a long time ago."

Just as the words left my mouth, I heard the low rumble of Zander's motorcycle pulling into my parking lot. Panic washed over me when my father stood and walked over to the window. As he looked down at the parking lot, a low, menacing chuckle vibrated through his chest. "Well, look who's here again. I shouldn't be surprised. The piece of shit thinks he owns the place ... and you."

"You're wrong, but I'm not going to waste my breath trying to convince you of something you'll never believe."

"I believe in facts, Delilah. And the fact is this guy is nothing but a piece of shit. What's that saying? You hang around shit long enough, you'll start to smell like it. Well, sweet Delilah, you're reeking of it."

"And what? You think you smell like roses? If anyone's reeking, it's *you*." I motioned my hand towards the door as I said, "I'm done with this insanity. This conversation is over. It's time for you to go."

"No. The conversation is over when I say it's over," he growled. "I came here for Danny, and I'm not leaving until I have him."

"What exactly do you want me to do here?"

"Call him. Tell him to meet us at Sully's in twenty minutes. Do whatever it takes to get him there, and tell him to come alone." When I hesitated, he barked, "Call him, Delilah. Now!"

Fearing what he might do, I reached into my purse and took out my phone. As I stared down at the screen, I knew I couldn't take the chance on Danny coming to the apartment, not when I didn't know what my father wanted with him, so I dialed Zander's number instead. My heart raced as I stood there waiting for him to answer. After just a few rings, I heard Zander's voice answer, "Delilah? Are you okay?"

"Hey, Danny. It's me. I need you to do me a favor."

"Danny?" Zander asked.

"Can you come meet me at Sully's?"

"I'm downstairs. I'm on my way up—"

"No, no," I interrupted him. "That's okay. You don't have to worry about it. I'll be fine. I just need to talk to you about something."

"*Delilah*." I could hear the concern in Zander's voice when he asked, "If you're in trouble, I'm coming up there!"

"I don't want to talk about this over the phone. Just meet me at Sully's in twenty minutes, and I'll tell you everything there.."

Relief washed over me when he said, "Okay, I got it."

"Good. Thank you."

"Can you stall whoever's there for a few minutes to give me some time to get the others here?"

"Yeah, no problem. I can do that." I glanced over at my father, and I prayed he was buying it as I asked Zander, "How long do you think you'll need?"

"Fifteen … twenty minutes tops."

"Okay, that'll be just fine."

"Shotgun and I are gonna leave the parking lot in case whoever's up there is watching, but I'll be just around the corner."

"Okay, that's fine. I'll wait a few minutes before I leave." Before I hung up the phone, I said, "Thanks, Danny."

As soon as the call ended, my father asked, "What did he say?"

"He's going to meet us, but it's going to take him longer than twenty minutes to get there." I put my phone back in my purse, then placed it on the table as I said, "It'll be a least forty-five minutes."

"Good. I knew I could count on you." His attention was drawn back to the window when Zander and Shotgun started up their bikes and pulled out of the parking lot. "Looks like your friends are leaving."

"I'm sure Zander thought I was asleep and decided to go home."

His eyes narrowed as he asked, "Hmm ... Is that right?"

"We had a disagreement earlier, and I'm sure he was hoping we could talk."

"A disagreement, huh?" he asked, still sounding skeptical.

"Yeah." I hoped I might be able to distract him from Zander by picking a fight with him. "As I recall, you and Mom had quite a few of those when I was growing up, usually over your spending all her money to pay off your gambling debts. How's all that going by the way? You still spinning the wheel, hoping for a big win?"

"My gambling days are over. I've moved on to bigger things."

"About that. How did you get involved in the whole dealing drugs thing anyway?"

"Same way Danny did. I ran into a little bad luck and needed a way to make some cash fast. Started doing a little dealing, but it didn't take me long to figure out that the big money was in running the show. That's when I decided to go into business for myself."

I could tell by the way he spoke that he took great pride in his accomplishment. Sadly, I couldn't have been less impressed. I didn't want him to know that, so I kept my face void of expression as I listened to him yammer on. "A man's gotta make a lot of sacrifices to make something out of nothing."

"What kind of sacrifices did you have to make, other than your wife and kids?"

"This conversation is growing old, Delilah." He stepped towards me as he said, "Let me see your phone."

"What? Why do you want my phone?"

"Give it to me, now!"

He reached over and grabbed my purse from the table. Panic washed over me as I watched him take out my phone. He went to my recent calls, then snarled, "*Fuck*. You called him. I should've known better than to trust you."

"So much for being smart."

I'd barely gotten the words out my mouth when the back of his hand met my cheek with a powerful slap. I quickly cowered away from him, cradling my throbbing jaw and busted lip in my hands. "You're about to learn that I'm not a man you want to cross, and the same goes for those bikers you've been running with."

He grabbed me by the arm, and as he started pulling me towards the door, I noticed a gun tucked away in his waistband. "Where are we going?"

"Getting the hell out of here before your friends show up."

With that, he opened the door and dragged me out into the hallway. I tried to pull free from his grasp, but he just tightened his grip and yanked me towards the emergency exit. Using his free hand, he opened the window, then stepped out onto the fire escape, pulling me behind him. I didn't bother asking why he hadn't gone out the front. I knew he was hoping to stay out of sight, but unbeknownst to him, Zander and Shotgun were parked just a few yards away, watching in silence as my father yanked me down the steps. It wouldn't be long before the rest of the Ruthless Sinners came to join them.

HAWK

When I saw Delilah being jerked down that fire escape, I wanted nothing more than to pull out my gun and put a bullet in the guy's head, but I couldn't take the chance of putting Delilah in even more danger. I had no idea if the guy was packing, and with Delilah stumbling down that metal staircase, I feared the guy might do something stupid. It was too dark to get a good look at him, but even from a distance, I knew I'd never seen the guy before. He was older, about my height with a medium build, and he was wearing dress pants, making it clear he was no fucking biker. I was watching them make their way down the last flight of stairs when I heard Shotgun ask, "Where the hell does he think he's taking her?"

"I have no idea, but I'm about to fucking find out."

As I got off my bike, Shotgun shook his head. "The brothers should be here any minute."

"We don't have time to wait. I got no idea where he's taking her."

"I get that but...."

"I'm going. Period."

"Then, I'm going with you." Shotgun got off his bike and said, "If nothing else, maybe we can stall him."

"We'll have to."

Shotgun followed me towards the alley. Delilah and the stranger had just stepped off the fire escape when the guy saw us walking in their direction. He reached behind him, and within a blink, he had the barrel of his gun pointed at Delilah's head. "Don't do something stupid, boys, or I'll end her right here."

"Easy, man. We don't want any trouble," I told him, stopping dead in my tracks. "Just let Delilah go, and we'll sort this thing out."

"You got another thing coming if you think I'm going to play games with the likes of you. Either back the fuck off, or I'm gonna pull the fucking trigger."

"It's okay, Zander. I'll be fine. Just do what he says," Delilah pleaded.

It wasn't until that moment when I noticed the red swelling across her cheek and her busted lip, and I was immediately consumed with rage. "He do that to you?"

"Yeah, I sure fucking did it," the man answered as he took hold of Delilah's hair, yanking her head back. "She's my daughter. I'll put her in her place whenever she fucking needs it."

Hoping to get him talking, I asked, "Your daughter?"

"You heard me. The name's Bruce Davenport, and yeah, this *whore* you've been fucking for the past month... is my *lovely daughter*." He gave Delilah's hair another hard tug, causing her to whimper in pain. I wanted to reach over and rip the guy's throat out. "Now, back the fuck off before you make me do something you'll regret."

"That's not gonna happen." I wanted to end the guy, but I knew the wrong move could cost Delilah her life, and I just couldn't take that chance. I took a step back and said, "Just tell us what you want, *Bruce*, and then we can settle this thing now before anyone gets hurt."

"He w-wants Danny," Delilah stammered. "You can't let him—"

Before she could finish, Delilah's father pulled her to his side, slamming his knee into her abdomen, knocking the breath out of her. I took a charging step towards them, as I growled, "You keep your fucking hands off her!"

I was just inches away from him when my stomach twisted into a knot at the familiar click of his gun's hammer. I had no choice but to stand there and listen helplessly as Delilah gasped for breath. "Best watch your step, boy, or you'll both end up dead."

"Look. Just let her go. We'll get Danny for you."

"It's too late for that." Bruce gave her a hard tug and said, "We're leaving, and if you know what's good for you, you'll move out of the fucking way."

Neither Shotgun nor I moved as Bruce started walking towards a red BMW that was parked in the back of her apartment. They hadn't made it very far when the roar of my brothers' bikes came rumbling down the alley as they pulled into the parking lot across from us. As soon as they parked and got off their bikes, the brothers started charging towards us, causing Delilah's father to panic. He quickly picked up his pace, tugging her further away from me. As the brothers got closer, I looked over to Viper and said, "It's Bruce Davenport ... Delilah's *father*, and he's got a gun on her."

"What the hell does he want with her?"

"That's just it," I quickly replied. "He doesn't want Delilah. He wants *Danny*."

About that time, Danny came up and asked, "Who wants me?"

"Your father," I answered. "He's the one who's got Delilah."

"You fuckin' kidding me?" Danny asked as he started down the alley. "If he wants me, then he can fucking have me, but he ain't gettin' Dee."

Danny rushed past us as he started running towards the back parking lot. Bruce was about to put Delilah in the car but quickly stopped when he heard Danny shout, "Yo, Dad! Hold up. It's me ... Danny. I'm here."

"Danny?"

Bruce turned back with surprise. He kept his gun pointed at Delilah as he watched Danny continue towards him. The brothers and I pulled out our weapons as we followed close behind him. Bruce seemed completely unfazed as we surrounded him. Danny tried to keep his cool as he asked, "What are you doing here?"

"I came looking for you. I thought you were in trouble." Bruce motioned his head towards Viper as he told Danny, "Figured these assholes had something to do with it."

"Why would you care if I was in trouble or not? I haven't seen you since I was kid."

"I had many reasons," Bruce answered. "You're not only my son, but one of my prized employees."

"Employee? What the fuck are you talking about?"

Confusion marked Danny's face as he stared at his father. "I don't work for you."

"That's where you're wrong. You've been working for me for the last several years."

"You're the boss?"

"The one and only," Bruce answered with a smug tone. "I noticed you weren't around for a few days. That wasn't surprising; it's happened before. But when Miller didn't return after his meet with you, I knew something was up. That's when I came to find you."

"So, what does Delilah have to do with any of this?"

"She was my way to you." Bruce glanced over to me as he continued, "When I didn't find you at your place, I went looking for her. I figured, in time, she'd lead me to you, but all she did was lead me to them. When I found out they were the ones selling my product in their strip club, I started piecing two and two together. It didn't take an Einstein to figure out that there was some connection between them and your sudden disappearance, and I'd bet my last dollar that they had something to do with Miller as well."

"Miller sold them trash. Took your money and half your take, so whatever happened to Miller, I'd say he got what he had coming." Danny's tone turned stronger, more determined as he said, "None of that matters now. If you're here for me, then you have me. Just let Delilah go, and let's end this shit."

"Danny, no," Delilah muttered. "You don't have to do this."

"Shut your fucking mouth!" Bruce gave Delilah a hard shove, knocking her to the ground. She was trying to pull herself up when he kicked her hard in the side. Seeing him hurt her again enraged me in a way I could never explain. My blood ran hot, like my very soul was on fire as I placed my finger on the trigger. I was about to end the motherfucker when Danny beat me to it. He reached behind and pulled his gun from the waistband of his jeans, and without a moment's hesitation, he fired, sending a bullet straight through his father's heart. Bruce's eyes widened in surprise as he looked down at his chest, watching in disbelief as blood started to seep through his shirt.

He stood there for a couple of beats before dropping down to his knees. "What have you done?"

"I just took my life back. My sister's too," Danny answered coldly. "I didn't want you in my life when I was a kid, and I sure as fuck don't now."

Bruce lifted his hand, aiming his gun at Danny, but before he had a chance to pull the trigger and end Danny, I fired off a shot at him, knocking him flat on his back. As the gun fell from his hands, Bruce mumbled, "Dead or alive. You'll always be my son. Nothing will change that."

Silence engulfed us as we all watched him take his last breath. Unable to stand it any longer, I rushed over to Delilah and knelt down beside her, pulling her into my arms. She quickly wrapped hers around me, pulling me close as she started to cry. I held her for a few moments before I finally whispered, "It's gonna be okay, Delilah."

"I'm so sorry for earlier. I shouldn't have put all the blame on you."

"You got nothing to be sorry about."

I was about to continue when Viper stepped over to us and asked, "She okay?"

"Yeah, she'll be fine."

"Well, I hate to rush, but we need to get moving." Viper glanced around Delilah's apartment complex. "By now, somebody's reported the gunshots, and the cops will be on their way."

"Okay. What do we need to do?"

"You tend to her. We'll take care of this."

Delilah's back stiffened as she watched Shotgun and Menace lift her father's body off the ground and carry it over to his BMW. Knowing I needed to get Delilah out of there, I turned back to Viper and asked, "You sure you got it covered?"

"Yeah, I've already put a call into Billy."

I nodded. "Thanks, Prez."

"No problem, brother. Go take care of your girl."

I quickly helped Delilah to her feet, and together we started walking towards the front of her apartment. We were about to go in when Danny rushed over. "Hey, Dee. Hold up a second."

"Danny." Tears started to fill Delilah's eyes once again as she asked, "Are you okay?"

"I'm fine. Don't worry about me." Remorse filled his eyes as he told her, "I'm really sorry about all this, Dee. I had no idea it was Dad I was working for."

"I know. He told me everything."

He glanced back over at his father's car, watching as the brothers locked his father away in the trunk. "I can't believe it was him, and that I actually killed him."

"I know it's hard, Danny, but—"

"No, that's just it. *It's not hard*, at least not as hard as it should be." Danny shook his head. "After all these years, he was still the same asshole that he was the day Mom walked out on him. I'd even go so far as to say he was worse."

"Yes. I can't disagree with you there. The man was clearly insane."

Danny lowered his head in shame as he muttered, "I should've never gotten involved in this shit. I'm going to make all this up to you, Dee. I swear it."

"Consider it a lesson learned." Delilah reached over and gave him a hug as she told him, "And just so you know, you're nothing like him. He might have been our father, but you're so much better than him. Remember that."

Danny gave her a slight smile as he replied, "I'll try."

"Hate to cut this short, guys, but we need to get moving." When Danny nodded, I told him, "Tell the guys to let me know if they need me."

"You got it."

Danny turned to head back to the others, and Delilah called out to him, "Hey! You need to call Mom. She's been—"

"I already took care of it," he interrupted. "I called her as soon as you left the clubhouse. Told her I'd be by the house tomorrow."

"Thanks, Danny."

"No problem."

I took Delilah by the hand and led her up the front steps of her apartment. Just as I opened the door, she turned to me and asked, "Do you mind if we stay at your place? I really don't want to be here tonight."

"Of course. Whatever you need, Delilah. I'm here for you."

She wound her arms around my neck, hugging me tightly as she whispered, "Thank you ... *for everything.*"

"There's nothing I wouldn't do for you, Delilah."

When she looked up to me, I leaned down and kissed her softly, careful not to hurt her busted lip, then rushed up to her apartment to grab a few of her things and the keys to her car. After being manhandled by her father, I doubted she'd be up for riding on my bike, so I called one of the prospects to come pick it up, and we took Delilah's car over to my place. On the way there, I couldn't stop glancing over at her, checking to see if she was really okay. Hearing the fear in her voice when she called me nearly broke me. I knew then, I would do anything to save her, and once I did, I would claim her as mine. Delilah was mine, and it was time everyone knew it—including her.

DELILAH

𝓘'd been at Zander's place several times over the past few weeks, but tonight there was something different about the modern four-bedroom Tudor-style home. Before, the sparse furniture and lack of home décor made the place seem cold and uninviting, but after everything that had happened, it felt safe and comforting. As soon as we walked in, I could feel the tension I was carrying start to ease, and I knew it had everything to do with Zander. He'd been so sweet to me, doing whatever he could to set my mind at ease—even going so far as to draw me a hot bath. Once it was ready, he came into the bedroom and took me by the hand, quietly leading me into the bathroom. His eyes never left mine as he slowly and ever so carefully started to remove my clothes. Anger marked his face when he removed my t-shirt and saw the bruising along my ribs. "I'm fine, Zander. It's just a couple of bruises. They'll go away in time."

"I want to kill him all over again for what he did to you."

"Zander, it's okay." I placed the palm of my hand on his cheek as I whispered, "He's gone. It's over."

He nodded, but the anguish in his eyes only grew more intense as he continued to remove my clothes. His touch was soft as he helped me undress. Once my clothes were gone, he guided me over to the bathtub. I slipped down into the warm, soapy water, and Zander knelt down on the floor next to me. He took a washcloth and dipped into the water, then soaped it up before gingerly running it across my back. I drew my legs up, resting my head on my knees and closed my eyes, relishing the feeling of the warm water cascading down my back. I tried not to think about my father or the events that had transpired earlier that night, but it wasn't long before the memories came rushing into my mind. My heart started to race as I thought about the moment I walked into my apartment and found my father sitting there in the dark. All the things he'd said to me caused my stomach to twist into a knot. I didn't want to believe that man was my father, that he could be so cold and cruel.

Unaware that I was working myself into a panic, Zander continued to bathe me, taking his time to wash my neck and down the length of my arms. I wanted to focus on his touch, but it was just too hard. I couldn't push the thoughts out of my head, and I started thinking about that moment when Danny pulled out his gun and shot him. Every muscle in my body tensed as I remembered the bullet piercing my father's chest and the look on his face when he realized he'd been shot. It was at that moment, Zander whispered, "Delilah ... are you okay?"

I fought back my tears as I turned to look at him and said, "No, but I will be."

"I love you, Delilah, and I'm here for you in any way that you need me. I hope you know that."

While he'd shown me in so many ways how he felt about me, he'd never actually said the words to me. Hearing them now only confirmed what I already knew. "I do know that, and I love you too, Zander. *So very much.*"

He leaned forward, gently pressing his lips to mine, and as he kissed me, I'd never felt so loved and adored. We sat there for several more minutes, talking about our versions of the night. I told him about the conversation my father and I had and all the threats he'd made, and how scared I was for Danny. I could hear the misery in his voice as he talked about watching my father and me coming down the fire escape. When he mentioned how he'd called the brothers, it brought back a thought I wanted to share with him.

"You know, when the guys showed and I realized they were there for me, I finally got what you've been talking about. I was starting to understand your draw to the club, especially after their visit with Mr. McClanahan, but tonight ... there was something really powerful about having your brothers come to my rescue like they did."

"I meant it when I said they'd do anything to protect you."

"I see that now."

I thought back to my conversation with my father and the anger I'd felt when he told me about the drugs. At the time, I didn't understand why I hadn't felt the same anger towards Hawk and his brothers. Now, I finally got it. Yes, the Ruthless Sinners did bad things. They sold drugs, ran strip clubs, and even killed bad people, but at the same time, they were good men. They had each other's backs at every turn and even risked their lives to keep their family safe. Zander was right when he told me his brothers weren't anything like my father. They'd proven that when they came to my rescue. It was that thought that had me wondering about the moment they loaded my father into the trunk of his car. Even though I knew it was doubtful he'd answer, I asked, "By the way, what will they do with my father?"

"You know I can't answer that. Just know it's been handled."

"By Billy?"

"*Delilah*," he warned.

"Okay, I'll leave it."

He helped me out of the tub and carefully dried me off, then he slipped one of his t-shirts over my head and led me into the bedroom. As he pulled the covers back, I looked around the room, noting once again the lack of furniture, and I couldn't stop myself from asking, "What's with the big house? You have three empty bedrooms, and just a few pieces of furniture in the rest of the house. Why haven't you done more with it?"

"Guess you could say I was waiting for you." He lifted his hands up to my face, brushing my cheek with the pad of his thumb. "I want you to make this house our home. Fill it with whatever you like."

My heart swelled with emotion as I looked up at him and saw the love in his eyes. I couldn't stop myself from lifting up on my tiptoes and kissing him once again. What started off as soft and tender, quickly became heated. I felt a warm rush of heat course through my body when his arms wrapped around me, pulling me close. Unfortunately, just as I was about to get lost in his touch, his arm pressed against my bruised ribs, causing me to whimper in pain. He quickly released me from our embrace, looking down at me with concern. "I'm sorry. I wasn't thinking."

"It's fine. I'm okay."

I went to reach for him but stopped when he shook his head. "You need your rest, Delilah. We have plenty of time for that once you've recovered."

"Zander, I'm—"

"This isn't up for debate."

With a determined look in his eye, he reached for the covers and lifted them, beckoning me to get into bed. As much as I wanted to protest, I gave in to his demands, and just as I'd hoped, he quickly removed his clothes and crawled in next to me. Even though I wanted to him to make love to me, it was comforting to have him nestled up close behind me. As I lay there listening to the soothing sound of his breath, my entire body started to relax, and it wasn't long before I drifted off to sleep.

The next morning, I was disappointed to find that I was in the bed alone. I'd hoped to pick up where we'd left off the night before, but that wasn't going to happen—not this morning or anytime soon, for that matter. Zander had his mind set on giving me time to heal. While urging me to stay in the bed and rest, he took care of all the cooking and everything around the house. The only time I even got out of my pjs was the day we rode over to the clubhouse.

Zander needed to speak with Viper about some club business, and he thought it would be a good opportunity for him to show me around. When we got there, most of the guys were off doing whatever it was they did, so the place was basically empty, giving us free rein to walk about. I'd only been in the one room when I was there before, so I had no idea how big the place really was. It was massive. Not only was there a full bar with pool tables and a jukebox, there was also a large kitchen and a family room area with sofas and a large flat-screen TV. I was surprised to see that there were enough bedrooms for every member to have their own room, and for the most part, they looked like the one I stayed in. Even though most of the guys had a place of their own, they used them whenever they wanted to spend the night at the clubhouse. Zander had me wait in the family room while he spoke with Viper, and as soon as they were done, Zander insisted that we return home.

I tried to protest, telling him I was fine and didn't need more rest, but he wasn't having it. He was set on taking care of me, and he did. In fact, he'd tended to my every need—except one. He refused to engage in any sexual activity whatsoever. Other than a few brief kisses, he simply wouldn't touch me, and even though I found it very endearing, I was becoming frustrated.

On the fourth morning, I'd had enough and decided it was time for us to talk. When I walked into the kitchen, he was wearing only his boxer briefs as he stood at the stove, frying up a batch of bacon. I took a moment to admire the defined muscles of his back. The man was a beautiful creature, and just looking at him had me wanting to reach out and touch him and spend the entire morning messing up the sheets with him. Unfortunately, when he glanced over his shoulder and saw how I was gawking at him, he shook his head and said, "Don't even think about, beautiful. We're not having any of that."

"And why not?"

"Because you've been through an ordeal and need time to heal."

"I've had time to heal, Zander. It's been days," I fussed. "The bruises are practically gone."

"You need more time." He turned his attention back to the stove. "Besides, we've got things we need to discuss."

"Such as?"

I walked over to the counter and sat down on one of the stools, listening with surprise as he said, "I want you to move in with me."

"What?" I gasped. "When?"

"The sooner the better." As if it were no big deal, he continued, "I was actually thinking I'd get a few of the prospects to bring the rest of your stuff over this afternoon."

"You don't think that's rushing it a bit?"

"Not at all." He turned to face me as he said, "I've waited a lifetime for you, and now that you're here, I don't want to waste a second of the time we have together."

"I don't know what to say."

A sexy smirk crossed his face as he said, "It's simple. Just say yes, and we'll start our future together."

"But—"

"Stop thinking of all the reasons why you should say no, and just say yes, Delilah." He leaned towards me, still smiling as he rested his elbows on the counter. "You know you want to."

"Are you sure about this?"

"Absolutely."

"Okay." I smiled. "I'll move in with you."

"That's my girl." He leaned in closer, briefly kissing me

before turning back to the stove. "I'll call the guys and get them to bring your stuff over."

"I have a lot of stuff, Zander. I'll want to be there to help."

"Fine, but I don't want you overdoing it and I'll be there to see that you don't."

"Okay, I guess that settles it. You have yourself a new roommate."

He glanced back over his shoulder as he said, "You'll be more than just a roommate, Delilah. You're my ol' lady, and if I have my way about it, it won't be long before you'll have my last name and a ring on that pretty, little finger of yours."

"Hold on there, Romeo. Don't you think you're moving a little fast with all this?"

"No, as a matter of fact, I don't." He pulled the skillet filled with scrambled eggs off the burner, then walked over to me. His eyes met mine as he said, "I don't know what I would've done if I lost you that night. I have no intention of finding out. Not now. Not ever."

"But I'm okay, Zander. You made sure of that. Your brothers too," I tried to assure him. "You don't have to worry anymore."

He reached for me, then kissed me long and hard, and when he was done, my entire body was humming with need. I inhaled a deep breath, and after I'd collected myself, I muttered, "Okay, I'm in."

"That's what I wanted to hear."

He kissed me once more, then went over to the stove and finished our breakfast. After we finished eating, he put a call in to the prospects and ordered them to go get my things. Keeping true to his word, they moved all my stuff over from my apartment, and I didn't have to lift a finger—until it came to unpacking everything they'd brought over. I took a week off from work and used the time to get things organized. I had the guys put my bedroom furniture in one of the empty bedrooms for a guest room and had them use my living room furniture to make an office out of one of the others. Once I started unpacking the rest of my things, it didn't take long before the place looked completely different. It looked like a home—our home.

When Zander came in from the clubhouse and saw everything I'd done, a proud smile crept over his face. "It looks great, babe."

"You think so?"

"Absolutely. Hell, I didn't even know it could look this good."

"I'm glad you like it."

"See? I was right. All this place needed was you."

As I stood there gazing at him, my mind was suddenly filled with wonderfully wicked thoughts. I walked over to him and took him by the hand, leading him into the bedroom as I said, "The bruises are gone."

"Is that right?"

He removed his cut and draped it over the dresser as I nodded with a smile. "I'm feeling really good. There's just one thing that would make me feel even better."

"You sure you're ready?"

A simple nod was all it took. As soon as he got the answer he needed, his mouth covered mine with a kiss that was hungry and demanding. I let my fingers trail along the curves of his perfectly defined chest and relished the sensation of having him so close. I felt him smile against my mouth as I reached for the hem of his shirt and eased it up over his head. My eyes drifted down, slowly roaming over the defined muscles of his chest, and I couldn't imagine wanting anyone more than I wanted him at that moment. "Zander."

"I'm right here, baby."

A moan of pleasure filled the room as his hands drifted down to my waist, pulling me tightly against his muscular frame. His warm hands slid beneath my tank top and across my bare back, his touch sending a rush of warmth through my entire body. I felt myself being led backwards as his strong hands slid up my waist, pulling the soft cotton fabric over my head. When the back of my legs touched the edge of the bed, he slowly lowered me down onto the mattress and tossed my shirt to the side. My breath became ragged with anticipation, my body begging impatiently for his next touch.

Zander looked down at me, watching appraisingly as my breasts rose and fell with each heaving breath. "You got no idea how hard it's been not to touch you. I've wanted you so fucking much."

"I've wanted you even more."

I gasped as his fingertips gripped my thighs and parted my legs to sink between them. When his hands cupped my breasts, I arched into them, as he lowered his head and trailed kisses across my chest. My ragged breaths echoed through the room as his hand slowly slid between my legs. He ran his thumb along the edge of my lace panties, teasing me and touching me where I wanted him the most. He took his time caressing me while his free hand cupped my breast, his soft lips hungrily nipping and sucking along the sensitive flesh. The rough, calloused pad of his finger stroked me as he growled, "So fucking perfect."

Zander alternated between my breasts, all while lowering my panties down my thighs. He tugged at them with agonizingly slow movements, reveling in the impatience building within me. My hands raked through his hair as I pulled his mouth closer. I could feel the smooth fabric of the lace slipping over my skin as my panties finally reached my ankles, and the storm of delicious sensations flooding through me were almost too much to bear. The warmth of his breath caressed my skin as he began to shower my stomach and thighs with kisses. My body began to tingle in anticipation as the bristles of his beard brushed against my center.

"Zander," I whimpered with need as my hands dropped to the sheets, clamping down. I felt his tongue sweep against me as his fingers eased inside me, and his tongue swirled around my most sensitive spot. As he continued to tease me with his mouth, I became lost in the sensation. I was close to the edge when my hands drifted to his head, my fingers tangling in his hair as I panted, "Yes," over and over again.

I was still in a haze when Zander lifted off me, reaching over to the bedside table for a condom. He was just about to roll it on when I said, "You don't need to ... I'm on the pill."

The words had barely left my mouth when he was back on top of me, centering himself between my legs. I smiled in satisfaction as his cock brushed against my clit, sending lust-filled chills down my spine. Our eyes met and everything stilled. In that moment there was no doubt in my mind that he loved me. I loved him too—

more than I ever dreamed possible and I had every intention of loving him like no one else could.

His lips pressed against mine as his warm hands roamed all over my naked body, leaving a trail of sparks in their wake. I opened my legs wider as he slowly slid inside me, making my breath catch in my throat. Seeing that I needed time to adjust, he stilled and kissed me along the curve of my neck and shoulder. Seconds later, my nails bit into his back as I rocked my hips against him, urging him to move. He pulled back and entered me again, slow and steady. Instinctively, I arched into him as he drove deeper, and I gasped as his cock rubbed against my G-spot. My body had never felt such unrelenting pleasure. He was everything I'd dreamt about and so much more. I'd found my home with him.

Zander's mouth once again found mine, and he kissed me hard as he thrust forward again and again, claiming what was his. Waves of ecstasy crashed over me until the dam finally broke and my body was flooded with the all-consuming rush of my climax. He continued to drive into me, deeper and deeper, until he found his own release. With one last thrust, a satisfied growl echoed through the room.

His breaths were ragged and deep as he dropped his head to my chest. With his hands drifting along the side of my hips and up to my waist, he whispered, "Mine."

The tips of my fingers lightly trailed the length of his back as I responded, "Yes, I'm yours."

He slowly rolled to his side, pulling me gently over him as his back fell against the mattress. I immediately curled into his side and rested my head on his shoulder. His fingers brushed through my hair as he said, "As much as I'd love to spend the rest of the night here in bed with you, the guys are meeting up at the new Stilettos later and I need to be there."

"Okay." I'd wondered about Stilettos from the start. I'd never been to a strip club before, and I was also curious to know more about that side of Zander's life. "Would you mind if I tag along?"

"You really want to?"

"Yeah, I've never been before." I gave him a slight shrug. "I'd like to see what all the fuss is about. Besides, if this club is going to be a part of your life, I want to be a part of it too."

"If you think you're gonna start stripping, you've got a another thing coming." I thought he was just teasing until he growled, "Your body is mine, and I'm not sharing it with anyone."

"No, Zander. I have no intention of stripping ... at least not unless I'm doing it for you and you alone." I giggled. "I just want to be a part of your life. That's all."

"Whatever you want, baby." He leaned down and kissed me on the forehead as he chuckled. "The girls are gonna love you."

"What does that mean?"

"You'll see."

HAWK

I was surprised when Delilah mentioned that she was interested in going to Stilettos with me, especially since she'd never been to a strip club before, but I wasn't going to deny her. Besides, I thought it would an interesting experience for us both. I would be able to see how things were going with the new product the club had purchased from Flint, and Delilah would get to spend some time with the brothers and experience for herself why so many came to our infamous strip clubs. She'd gotten all dolled up in one of her little black dresses that clung to her curves with a pair high heels. Her hair was curled and down around her shoulders, and it was difficult to keep my hands off her as we started towards the front door.

Before we went in, I considered warning Delilah that she would be entering a different world, much different than what she'd seen on TV, but I decided against it, choosing to let her see for herself. I held the door open and watched as her eyes widened with surprise as she stepped inside. The spotlights were flashing, the music was blaring, and you could almost smell the scent of lust and fantasy that hung in the air. Delilah weaved through the slew of people like a pro, smiling as she noticed how hyped up they were to see the women dancing on the stage. There were five different stages in the new club, each one with its own lighting system and stream of beautiful women who could charm a twenty-dollar bill out of any man's hand. Delilah took her time making her way through the crowd, and as soon as she spotted the guys sitting at one of the back tables, she turned to me and smiled. "You want to go over and sit with them?"

"Yeah, that'd be good."

I took her by the hand and led her over to the table, and as soon as we approached, the brothers stood to welcome Delilah. A bashful smile crossed her face as she said, "Thanks guys. It good to see you too."

"You want a drink?"

"Sure."

"Whatcha want?"

Delilah sat down next to Axel and said, "A Long Island iced tea would be nice."

"You got it." I called over to Misty, one of the waitresses, and placed our order, then sat down next to Delilah. I glanced over at Viper and said, "Looks like another big night."

"It is." He leaned in as he whispered, "Product is moving well. Looks like Flint is a go."

"Good to hear."

He nodded, then turned his attention to Delilah. "How you been making it?"

"Much better, thanks to you guys." Emotion filled her

eyes as she said, "I never got a chance to thank you for coming to help me out with my father."

"Glad to do it."

"I also wanted to thank you for deciding to give Danny another chance. I wasn't expecting you to let him go, but I'm really glad you did."

"No need to thank me." Being vague at best, Viper told her, "Danny earned his way out."

"Well, I appreciate it just the same."

Misty brought over our drinks, and after she placed Delilah's cocktail on the table, she touched her shoulder and smiled, "I love your dress."

"Thank you." Delilah's eyes skirted over Misty's skimpy miniskirt and halter top as she replied, "I like yours too."

"You're really pretty." Misty reached for a strand of Delilah's hair, twirling it in her fingers as she purred, "I just *love* your hair."

The guys were completely captivated by the scene that was unfolding before them, watching Misty as she flirted with Delilah. Slightly thrown by her advances, Delilah simply replied, "Thank you. That's really sweet of you to say."

"I'll be available if you want a dance later."

Delilah's eyes widened in surprise. Not knowing how to answer, she turned to me, hoping for a rescue. I was enjoying watching her squirm, so I simply smiled, forcing her to fend for herself. Delilah finally glanced over at Misty and said, "Thanks, but I'm with Hawk."

"That's okay. He can join us." Misty leaned forward, her breasts right in Delilah's face as she whispered, "The more the merrier."

"Come on, Delilah," Rafe taunted. "You wouldn't want to let the girl down, now would ya?"

Delilah cut her eyes over at Rafe as if looks could kill and answered, "Maybe later. I have a drink to finish."

"Okay. I'll be around. Just let me know when you're ready."

When she turned and walked away, the brothers started rolling in laughter.

Delilah shook her head and then reached for her drink and took a long sip. Rafe wasn't about to let an opportunity to tease her pass him by, so he leaned over to her and said, "Misty's got some real talent. You might learn something from her. I'm sure Hawk would appreciate it."

They guys started rolling once again, and when I noticed that spark in Delilah's eyes, I knew she was about fire back at him. She placed her drink on the table, then brushed her hair away from her face. "Just so you know, I have a few talents of my own. Misty would be lucky to learn them from me."

"I'm sure she would," Rafe snickered.

"And you're an ass."

"Sure am, but you can't blame me. Girl on girl action is hot."

"Um-hmm. Just remember"—a mischievous smile crossed Delilah's face—"payback's a bitch."

"Bring it on, sister!" Rafe teased.

Delilah was just about to respond when Sydney, one of the club's dancers came over to the table. She was tall and slender with a set of fake tits and platinum-blonde hair that draped down her back. Sydney was wearing a small sequined bikini, and it didn't take long to figure out that she had her sights set on Delilah. "Hey there. You having a good time?"

"Yes, I am." Delilah answered as her eyes skirted over to the guys. Once again, their total focus was on her. "The guys are too, but umm ... Rafe over there, he's feeling a little lonely. You see, his ol' lady dumped him because he isn't very good in the sack."

"Oh, really?" Sydney looked over at Rafe with pity in her eyes. "I would love to help him out with that."

"Hold the fuck up," Rafe fussed. "I don't need any help. I'm actually pretty fucking phenomenal in bed, thank you very much."

The guys busted out in laughter when Delilah leaned over to Rafe and teased, "Come on, Rafe. You wouldn't want to let the girl down, now would ya?"

"Fuck y'all." Rafe stood up and took Sydney by the hand, leading her towards the back. "I'll show her. Just wait and see."

Once they were gone, Delilah looked over to me and asked, "Did I go too far?"

"Ah, hell no. Rafe totally had that shit coming." A pleased smile crossed her face when I told her, "You got him good."

"I thought so too."

Viper nudged me with his elbow as he said, "The girl's got spunk. I like her. I think it's safe to say we all do."

"Good, 'cause I plan on her sticking around."

Viper gave me a nod of approval, then ordered us all another round of drinks. We all continued talking. Delilah had finished off her second Long Island and was well on her way with the third, and it was clear by the way she was swaying in her seat that she was feeling pretty good.

Since she was enjoying herself, I used the opportunity to check in with Menace. He'd been monitoring the sale of the new product, and I was eager to see how it was going. I leaned over to her as I said, "I need to see about something. You gonna be okay for a minute?"

"Sure." She reached for her drink, taking a sip from the straw as she looked over to the stage, watching as one of the girls made her way over to the pole. Her words were slurred as she told me, "You know, these girls are real-leee tahhlented. I could never swing around on that thing like they can."

"Hang tight, beautiful. I'll be right back."

I motioned over to Shotgun, telling him to keep an eye on Delilah, then headed up front to the office. When I walked in, Menace was busy counting cash. "How's it going?"

"Better than expected. Looks like this shit is even better than what we were getting from Danny."

"Viper said the same. Glad it's paying off."

"No doubt. So, how's it going out there on your end?"

"Good. Decided to bring Delilah along."

"Really?"

"Yeah." I chuckled as I told him, "She'd never been to a strip club and wanted to see for herself what all the fuss was about."

"And how's she liking it?"

"Seems to be having a good time. The girls certainly seem to like her."

Menace smirked. "I bet they do."

Our attention was drawn over to the door when Zoe stuck her head in the doorway and asked, "Hey, Menace ...You got a minute?"

Zoe was one of our dancers. She was young with a kid, trying to do what she could to put food on the table, and Menace, apparently, had a soft spot for her. "Yeah, doll. Whatcha need?"

When she glanced over at me, I knew she wanted to talk to him alone, so I said, "I'm gonna head out, brother. I'll see ya at the clubhouse in the morning."

"See ya then."

On my way out, I closed the door behind me and headed back to find Delilah. I hadn't gotten very far when I felt someone tug at my arm. When I turned around, I was surprised to see that it was Lisa. I knew Viper had brought her over to get the bar up and running, but I thought it was only going to be for a few days. She stepped towards me, placing the palms of her hands on my chest with a seductive smile. "Hey there, handsome stranger. How have you been making it?"

"Good. Really good. How about yourself?"

"I've been doing okay. I was hoping that you'd change your mind and take me up on my offer. I'm free later tonight if you're up for it."

Just like the time before, I wasn't interested in hooking up with her. Not now. Not ever. "Sorry, Lisa. That's not gonna happen."

"Oh come on, Hawk. It's just one night." She inched a little closer. "I'm sure we'd have ourselves a real good time. One to put in the books."

Before I could respond, Delilah popped up at my side. She was having a little trouble keeping her footing, so she reached for my arm to keep herself from stumbling. I knew then that I shouldn't have ordered her that third drink. It was more than evident that the alcohol had taken effect when Delilah leaned towards Lisa and slurred, "I'm sssorry to disappoint ya, sweetheart, but this one's taken."

Lisa's brows furrowed in irritation. "*What?*"

"He's *miiine*." Delilah started to sway a bit, so I slipped my arm around her waist, holding her up as she said, "You can't have him."

Lisa turned to me with a soured expression. "Is she being serious right now?"

"*Hell, yeah*. I'm being ser-*ious*." Delilah held out her hand, trying in vain to point her finger at Lisa as she said, "Look ... I'm sure you're a lovv-ly girl and all, but you need to ... back ... the ... fuckkkk ... *off*."

Lisa looked over to me. "You two have fun."

When she huffed away, Delilah's expression quickly grew solemn. "I don't think she likes me very much."

It took all I had not to laugh at Delilah's possessive display. I knew it was just the alcohol talking, letting her insecurities shine through. I leaned down and kissed Delilah on the temple and said, "I think it's time for us to go."

"What?" Delilah looked over to me with a pout. "It's still early."

"You know, if we stick around much longer, Misty is gonna come looking for you about that *lap dance*."

Delilah's eyes widened, "I don't wanna lap dance, and she's got another thing coming if she thinks she's gonna give you one ... or me one with you ... or both of us together with her, 'cause that's not gonna happen."

"Yeah, you've definitely had too much to drink."

"Definitely," she agreed. "I usually only have one ... maybe two at the most. Nevver threee."

"Then, let's get out of here. I'll catch up with the guys tomorrow."

As we headed out to the parking lot, Delilah had to hold on to me to keep her footing, making me glad we'd decided to take her car instead of my bike. Once I had her settled in the passenger seat, I got in next to her, and we started home. Delilah's eyes were closed as she muttered, "It wasn't what I expected."

"I didn't figure it would be."

"There's a lot of temptation there ... *like a lot.*" Her words came painstakingly slow, and I knew she was close to falling asleep as she said, "So many pretty girls ... and they have these great bodies and amazing boobs. No way I can compete with that."

"There is no competition, Delilah. You're the only woman I want."

"You say that now"—her head rolled towards me and she opened her eyes—"but when I'm pregnant and fat with crazy hormones and swollen feet, you might change your mind."

We'd never actually talked about having kids, but the thought of Delilah being the mother of my children couldn't have pleased me more. "You want kids?"

"I want your kids," she answered without hesitation. "One or two, but three would be okay too."

"I can't imagine a more beautiful sight than seeing you carrying my kid."

Her eyes closed once again. "I'll remind you that you said that when I'm waddling around the house and I'm too fat to put on my own shoes."

"I won't need reminding. Damn. You'll look so fucking hot, I won't be able to keep my hands off of you."

When she didn't respond, I glanced over and noticed she'd fallen sound asleep, leaving me no choice but to continue our conversation later. When we got back home, she never woke up as I carried her inside and put her to bed. While I was glad she'd had a good time at the club, I had no doubt she'd regret that third drink in the morning. I didn't realize how much so until the following morning.

I was sitting in the kitchen talking to Danny when Delilah came dragging into the room with a pained groan. There were dark circles under her eyes, her hair was a tangled mess, and she looked like she was on her last leg as she hobbled over and sat down on one of the stools. As soon as she was seated, she planted her elbows on the counter and dropped her head in hands. "I think I'm dying."

"Damn, Dee. I heard you had a good time last night, but I didn't realize you'd had *that* good of a time." Danny teased.

"Can you not talk so loud?" Delilah grumbled. "My head is pounding."

I reached into the cabinet for a couple of Tylenol, then grabbed a large bottle of water out of the fridge. I slid them over to Delilah and said, "Take these. It'll help."

"I think I showed out last night... acted a damn fool." She tossed the pills in her mouth, then washed them down with a long drink of water. "I don't know what I was thinking."

"Don't worry about it. After everything you've been through, you deserved a night out," Danny tried assure her. "I know you're hungover now, but have you been making it all right?"

Danny had called every day, checking in to making

sure she was handling things with her father. She'd tried to assure him that she was okay, but he had his doubts. He wasn't the only one. I'd been worried about her, too. It had to be difficult for her to watch her brother kill their father, but just like the times before, Delilah answered, "I'm okay."

"Are you really?" Danny pushed.

"Yes. Really." Delilah lifted her head and looked over to her brother. "I'll admit this whole thing with Dad has messed with my head, just as much as it's messed with yours, but he was never really a father to either of us. He was more like a wound that wouldn't heal, but now that he's gone, maybe we can finally put him behind us and move on."

"Maybe so, but I'm still pissed about it all. I really hate him for all the shit he's done."

"You have your whole life ahead of you. Don't let him tarnish that." Delilah tried her best to smile. "Besides, you know what they say, 'The best revenge is a well-lived life.'"

"I can't disagree with you there." Danny glanced at me and said, "Since you brought it up, Hawk and I have been talking about my future. The brothers have offered me a chance to prospect for them, and I'm thinking I'm gonna take them up on it."

"Seriously?"

"Yeah, seriously. It's been good spending these past couple of weeks with them. I get the whole draw to the club life, and I really think it would give me some direction."

"I think that sounds great, Danny. I'm really happy for you."

"Me too." Danny reached over and gave her a hug. "I'm

gonna get out of here and let you nurse that hangover. If you need me, just give me a shout."

"I will." As he started for the door, Delilah told him, "I love ya, Danny."

"Love you too."

Once he was gone, I made Delilah some breakfast, hoping it would settle her stomach, and it seemed to do the trick. By the time she was done eating, her color was back, and she was actually moving about without groaning. In hopes of shaking the remains of her hangover, she decided to take a shower. When she came out, I was waiting for her in the bedroom. "Feeling better?"

"Much."

"I wanted to ask you ... Do you remember our conversation on the way home last night?"

"I think so." She took the towel off her head and shook out her damp hair. "You mean the one about the girls at the club?"

"Yeah, that'd be the one."

"Well, I was pretty tipsy at the time, so don't hold it against me."

"I've always been a firm believer that alcohol has a way of making the truth come out." Her eyes met mine as I continued, "I meant it when I said you're the only woman I want, Delilah. Now and forever."

She walked over to me, positioning herself between my legs as she placed her hands on my face. "And you're the only man I want."

When she leaned in to kiss me, I pulled her onto the bed with me, and I spent the rest of the morning showing her just how much I wanted her, and I intended to continue showing her until the day I took my last breath.

EPILOGUE

Three months later

It couldn't have been a more perfect day for a ride. The sun was shining bright, there was a cool breeze, and not a cloud in the sky. I had my brothers at my side and my woman at my back, and the roar of our engines was like music to my ears. We'd just started around the first of three hundred and eighteen curves of the Dragon's Tail when Delilah tightened her grip around my waist. She'd never admit it, but I knew she was feeling a little leery. I couldn't blame her. While I'd been down the road many times in my life, it was a first for Delilah. She was doing her best to hold her own, but it was a dangerous roadway, especially for a novice rider like her. I tilted my head back as I asked her, "You doing okay?"

"Yep, I'm great."

I nodded, then eased back on the throttle and leaned into the next big curve.

I would've waited until she had a little more experience riding before I took her on a ride like this, but she insisted, assuring me that she could handle it. She glanced behind us and said, "They go on for miles."

I nodded as I glanced over to my sideview mirror, noting not only all the Ruthless Sinners, but the line of Dark Ravens as well. There was no denying, that together, we made one hell of a group. We'd made it halfway up the eleven-mile run when Big Ben, the president of the Dark Ravens pulled up next to Viper and gave him the nod, letting him know it was time. We all slowed, giving him a chance to prepare. Once he'd gotten the urn out of his saddlebag, he made his way to the back of the group. As soon as Big Ben was in position at the rear, he removed the top of the urn and held it in the air. We were all moved by the sight of McClanahan's ashes scattering in the wind. Knowing how much he enjoyed riding this particular trail, we couldn't think of a better way for him to spend eternity.

The group was somber as they paid their respects to a lost brother, and the feeling continued as we rode up to Deals Gap Motorcycle Resort. We'd made arrangements to eat there together before heading back to Nashville. Once we were all parked, we gathered in one of the larger seating areas and listened as Big Ben spoke a few words about McClanahan. By the time he was done, there was barely a dry eye in the place. When it was time to load up and head back home, Big Ben came over to speak to Delilah. "I just wanted to thank you for all you did for Cap'. He thought a lot of you."

"I thought a lot of him as well. I know today would've meant the world to him."

"Wish we could've done more when he was alive. The ornery bastard gave us a hell of a time whenever we came around, but I got it. I knew he didn't want us to see him like that."

"I'm sure it wasn't easy on him, but it didn't change the fact that you and your brothers meant everything to him."

Big Ben glanced over his shoulder, and when he saw that his brothers were waiting on him, he turned back to us and said, "I best get going. If you guys ever need anything, all you gotta do is call."

"Will do."

He gave us both a hug, and then left to join his brothers. As they started rolling out, Delilah looked up at me and said, "Today was amazing. Thank you for putting it all together."

"You're welcome, but I didn't do it for you." I smiled as I told her, "I wanted him to get his last ride."

"Well, it was incredible. I can definitely see why they call it the Dragon's Tail." I could hear the excitement in her voice when she said, "Those curves are insane."

"You liked them, huh?"

"Definitely. I can't wait to ride them again." She glanced over at Danny. He was standing by his bike talking to the other brothers. "Looks like Danny enjoyed it too. I still can't get used to seeing him in that prospect cut."

Danny had been prospecting for just under three months, but he'd already shown himself to be an asset to the club. He knew how to take orders without question and never failed to be present when he was needed. "He wears it well."

We were both looking over at him and the others when Viper came up to us and asked, "You two ready to head back?"

"Whenever you are, Prez."

"Thank you for doing this with us today." Delilah reached up on her tiptoes and kissed Viper on the cheek. "It meant a lot to me, and I know it meant a lot to Mr. McClanahan."

"Anything for a fellow brother." He gave her a wink, then said, "Now, let's head on home while we still have some daylight left."

As soon as Viper gave the word, we all got on our bikes and made the trek back. It was late when we got home, and after such a long ride, I figured Delilah would've been ready to call it a night. I was wrong. We'd just started to undress for bed when she got that look in her eye. I was standing there in my boxer briefs when she walked over to me and asked, "You tired?"

"Not that tired. Why? Whatcha got on your mind?"

She placed her hands on my chest, lifting up on her tiptoes as she pressed her lips against mine, leaving no question to what she had in mind. I was all in. Having her so close set me on fire. Feeling the heat surge through me, my hand dove into her hair, pulling her close as I deepened the kiss. I was quickly losing control, and Delilah knew it. Breaking from our embrace, she let her fingers trail slowly down my abdomen. With the waistband of my boxers in hand, she lowered herself to her knees.

As I watched her kneel, my cock instantly hardened. I held her gaze as I stepped out of my boxers and waited for her to make her next move. My entire body craved her touch, and I ached with anticipation. With one hand, she took me in her fist and firmly squeezed me in her palm. Her other hand slid up my thigh, gently cupping my balls as her mouth closed over the head of my throbbing cock. Fuck. Her warm, soft skin against mine and the wet heat of her mouth were almost too much for me to take, and I had to work to steady myself. A sudden groan escaped me as I savored the feeling of those talented lips around my cock and the flood of sensations wracking my body as she began to move her tongue.

This woman exceeded every fantasy I'd ever had. She took me deeper into her mouth until my cock pressed against the back of her throat. I could feel my orgasm building, winding me tighter and tighter, as she hungrily sucked and licked my cock.

As much as I loved her mouth on me, I needed to be inside her, so I reached down and quickly lifted her to her feet. My tone was rough when I growled, "On the bed, Delilah."

Her eyes locked on mine, then she did what she was told. Fuck. She looked so damn beautiful sprawled out on the bed, bare and waiting for me with that wanton look in her eyes. I crawled on top of her, quickly removing her satin panties and spread her legs wide as I settled between them. Her breathing became uneven and hitched as I brushed my throbbing cock against her center. "You want my cock, baby?"

"Yes, Zander. Yes."

As soon as the words left her mouth, I drove deep inside her, giving her exactly what she wanted. She wrapped her legs around me, forcing me deeper inside. I froze. She felt too fucking good. As I slowly withdrew, I looked down at her. Her eyes were clouded with desire and pleasure. "I love you, Delilah. Every fucking inch of you."

The room stilled as she placed the palms of her hands on my chest and whispered, "I love you too. More than you'll ever know."

"Show me how much you love me," I demanded.

And she did. Over and over again.

ACKNOWLEDGMENTS

I am blessed to have so many wonderful people who are willing to give their time and effort to making my books the best they can be. Without them, I wouldn't be able to breathe life into my characters and share their stories with you. To the people I've listed below and so many others, I want to say thank you for taking this journey with me. Your support means the world to me, and I truly mean it when I say I appreciate everything you do. I love you all!

PA: Natalie Weston

Editing/Proofing: Lisa Cullinan-Editor, Rose Holub-Proofer, Honey Palomino-Proofer

Promoting: Amy Jones, Veronica Ines Garcia, Neringa Neringiukas, Whynter M. Raven

BETAS/Early Readers: Tanya Skaggs, Jo Lynn, and Jessey Elliott

Street Team: All the wonderful members of Wilder's Women (You rock!)

Best Friend and biggest supporter: My mother (Love you to the moon and back.)

A short excerpt of Prospect: Satan's Fury MC-Memphis Book 8 is included in the following pages. Blaze, Shadow, Riggs, Murphy, Gunner, Gus, Rider and Prospect are also included in this Memphis series, and you can find them all on Amazon. They are all free with KU.

# EXCERPT FROM PROSPECT: SATAN'S FURY MC-MEMPHIS

PROSPECT

"It's not just about knowing the brothers' names and their position in the club. You gotta know *everything* about them," Rider explained. "Their backgrounds ... where they grew up, jobs they've had, past experiences. What their life was like before joining the club ... and after—the good, the bad, and the ugly."

Rider had been chosen by Gus to be my sponsor. It was his job to guide me through prospecting and make sure I knew everything that would be expected of me during the process. Feeling overwhelmed by what he'd just informed me, I turned to him and asked, "I hear what you're saying, but I don't get why it matters so much. I mean, what difference does it make if I know what jobs Blaze had as a kid?"

"It's knowing what your family is all about," Rider answered firmly. "Knowing that Cyrus and T-Bone were here with Gus when he first started up the Memphis chapter and how they helped him find the clubhouse and build our numbers. And knowing that when our brother

Runt was killed, Shadow was the one who stepped up to the plate and saved our asses, earning our vote as the club's new enforcer. It helps you understand where the brothers have been ... where they're going. It gives you some insight to what makes them tick."

"I get that, but how am I supposed to find out all this shit?"

"You listen ... not only to what they say, but what they don't say." Rider looked me directly in the eye. "You'll get it. It's just going to take time."

I hoped Rider was right. I wanted to think that I had what it took to earn my patch, but there were times when I wasn't so sure. If I wanted to be considered family to these men, I had a lot of work to do, and it wasn't going to be easy. There were over thirty members I had to learn about, all the while doing the other crazy bullshit that came along with prospecting. But I wasn't complaining. I'd finally found the life I wanted, and I wasn't going to let anything stand in my way. I gave Rider a slight nod and answered, "I'll do whatever I gotta do."

"I know you will." He lifted his beer. "I'll help where I can."

"I'd appreciate that, brother."

Just as the words left my mouth, Darcy, Rider's ol' lady, came walking into the living room. I could still remember the first time we'd met. I'd only been in Memphis for a few days when the brothers hired her to be the garage's custom painter. There weren't many women who could handle working in a shop full of strong-willed bikers, but she managed it like a pro. Darcy and Rider had grown up in the same small town and had history. It didn't take long for them to pick up where they left off, and they'd been inseparable since. Rider and I were sitting on the sofa when she walked over with a concerned expression on her face. "You know, we could go to the Smoking Gun with Murphy and the others tonight. I can hit one of Brannon's shows another time."

"I'm good with going to Neil's to see him tonight," Rider told her. "With the crowd that'll be at the Smoking Gun, it's not like they'll miss us."

"I know, but I don't want to disappoint Riley."

"I already talked to Murphy. It's all good, babe."

Looking relieved, she smiled and said, "Good. I just wanted to be sure."

"What's the big deal with the Smoking Gun anyway?"

Rider turned to me as he explained, "Riley and the owner of the bar, Grady, are first cousins and best friends, and he's having some big shindig tonight for the playoffs. I'm kind of glad we decided not to go. I wasn't looking forward to fighting that crowd."

"Okay, then I guess it's about time for us to head over to Neil's. Brannon's show starts at eight," Darcy said.

Taking our cue, Rider and I got up and followed her outside to our bikes. I waited as she got settled behind him, then we both fired up our engines and headed downtown. As we made our way towards Neil's bar, I was feeling pretty good about things in my life, and I found myself thinking of the day Viper had come to me about leaving Nashville and staying with Satan's Fury. I couldn't blame him for wanting to get me out of town. I was a ticking time-bomb. Every time something didn't go my way, I'd blow up and do something stupid—get into a fight or be laid-out drunk. When I landed myself in trouble with the law again, my mother freaked out and called Viper for help.

I KNEW the second I walked out of that jailhouse and found him standing in the parking lot he was pissed. I wasn't surprised. I'd fucked up once again, and he was the one who'd pick up the pieces so my mother wouldn't have to.

Once we were inside his truck, Viper turned to me with a fierce expression. "This shit has got to stop, Clay."

"I know."

"If you know, then what are you going to do about it?"

"I don't know." I shrugged. "I'll figure something out."

"Yeah, you've been dishing out that same bullshit ever since the night you beat the hell out of that kid, and I'm tired of hearing it," he growled. "I feel for you, Clay. I really do. I know you've had some rough blows, but it's time for you to make a change ... a real change."

I couldn't argue. He was absolutely right. It was time for me to change, to pull my head out of my ass and get my life back on track, but I had no idea how I was going to make that happen. "I know. I'm trying."

"You're obviously not trying hard enough!" He paused for a moment, and once he'd collected himself, his tone was softer. "I've got an old friend ... He's got a club down in Memphis. I think you should go down and try to prospect for him."

"Wait ... what?" From the day he joined the Ruthless Sinners, Viper had dedicated his life to his brothers. Hell, he lived and breathed for them, so I was surprised when he'd suggested I prospect for an MC that wasn't his. "If I was going to prospect for a club, why wouldn't I just do it for you and the Sinners?"

"I considered that, and honestly, I think you'd do well with us." I could see the sincerity in his eyes. "But there are too many memories here ... too many things holding you back. It's time for you to get a fresh start, and I think you can accomplish that with Satan's Fury. Gus is a good man ... runs a tight ship with a good group of men."

"So, what are you expecting me to say here?" To say that I was resistant to the idea was putting it lightly. In fact, the entire thing seemed ludicrous to me, and even though Viper was a very powerful man, I wasn't shy about letting him know exactly how I felt. My words dripped with sarcasm as I continued, "Sure. I'll pack up my shit and move to fucking Memphis."

"Yeah. That's exactly what I expected you to say," he said. "Actually, I'm not taking any other answer. I've already spoken with Gus, so get yourself prepared because you're heading out at the end of the week."

I could tell by his tone that he wasn't going to take no for an answer, so I just swallowed my pride and kept my mouth shut. I thought if I just gave him time to cool down that I could talk him out of it later. I was wrong. Viper wasn't giving up on the idea. At the end of the week, he showed up at the house, and the anger that lingered so close to the surface started to rise up once again. I was just about to blast him, tell him to go to hell and refuse to leave, but then I noticed the expression on my mother's face. The concern in her eyes hit me like a ton of bricks. My actions had hurt her, and that was the last thing I wanted to do. So, as Viper requested, I packed my shit and drove to Memphis. As soon as I walked through the clubhouse doors, a strange sensation washed over me. The hostility and heartache that had been weighing on me suddenly seemed to fade into the background.

. . .

At the time, I didn't know why. I thought it might've been because I was so focused on trying not to make an ass of myself in my newfound surroundings, but as the weeks passed, I started to realize it was much more than that.

I was still thinking about the first time I'd met Gus when Rider, Darcy, and I pulled up at Neil's. It was about half the size of the Smoking Gun, but that didn't stop the crowds from rolling in. It was a happening place. There was a stage and lighting for their live bands, a dance floor, and plenty of tables for those who just wanted to sit and drink their beer while listening to some great local talent —including this Brannon Heath guy who Darcy wanted to see. I'd never heard of him, but Darcy was a huge fan, particularly of the latest song he'd written. As soon as we were inside the bar, Darcy led us over to a table close to the stage, and it wasn't long before one of the waitresses came over to take our drink orders. She was older, maybe in her late forties, and while she tried to hide it, I could tell by the dark circles under her eyes that she'd already had a long night. With a slight smile, she looked down at us and asked, "What can I get you folks tonight?"

"A round of whatever you have on tap would be great," Rider answered.

"You got it."

When she turned and headed over to the bar, I took a quick glance around and noticed how everyone in the room seemed to be having a great time. Unfortunately, I didn't feel the same. I couldn't stop thinking about all the stuff I needed to learn about the brothers. I'd never been a stellar student and was afraid I wouldn't be able to get it all down. The fear of failure was daunting, so much so, I not only missed that the waitress had brought our drinks over, but that the band had already taken their place on the stage. A bright smile crossed Darcy's face when Heath stepped up to the microphone. "Hey ... there he is. I think they're about to start."

I nodded as I reached for my beer and took a quick sip. As much as I wanted to down the whole damn thing, I knew I couldn't—not while I was prospecting. There was always a chance that one of the brothers would need me, so like it or not, I had to keep my senses intact. Trying to make the best of it, I leaned back in my seat and listened as the band started to play. After a few songs, I could see why Heath was becoming such a big hit in the city. The guy had a good voice, and his lyrics weren't so bad either. I could've sat there and listened to the band all night, but just as I was really starting to settle in, my burner rang. I reached into my pocket with a nagging suspicion that I was being beckoned by one of the brothers. I looked down at the screen, and just as I thought, it was a message from Riggs. He was having some bike trouble and needed a hand. Knowing I couldn't keep him waiting, I motioned to Rider, letting him know that I was leaving, and headed out the door. As I got on my bike, I wasn't feeling aggravated or put out. I knew with each time the brothers called me for help, I was one step closer to becoming a member of Satan's Fury, and there was nothing I wanted more.

LANDRY

There were those girls in high school who'd always seemed to have it all—the ones with the perfect figure, perfect hair, and flawless skin. They could eat anything they wanted to without gaining a single pound, and for whatever reason, everyone on the planet seemed to absolutely adore them. Yeah, I hadn't been one of those girls. I was five-foot-ten and wore a size twelve, so I was far from little. My hair had been a curly, frizzy mess, and my complexion a total nightmare. It wasn't that I hadn't attempted to make myself look better, I did. I used all the hair mousses and gels, doctored my breakouts, and had tried every fad diet known to man. It didn't matter though. There'd been nothing I could do to make myself stand out in the crowd—at least, not while Mom was around.

My mother had been the vice principal of my high school, and a complete knockout. There wasn't a guy around who hadn't noticed her great curves, especially when she'd been wearing one of her tight pencil skirts—

and to make matters worse, the guys who I'd desperately hoped would notice *me* were constantly telling me how hot they thought my mom was. It'd been soul crushing. No matter how hard I had tried, I was forever hidden in her shadow. If that wasn't enough, I also had to contend with my brother and his enormous popularity. Jacob was not only a big guy—six-seven and two hundred and eighty pounds—he'd also been a star athlete. He played football, basketball, and baseball, and he played them well. Everyone in town had thought he was the greatest thing since sliced bread, including my parents, and my only claim to fame had been the fact that I was his sister.

I'd hoped things would change after I graduated and went off to college. They hadn't. I never could shake those inferior feelings from my childhood. I'd gotten my degree without ever taking any real risks, figuring I wouldn't get rejected or hurt if I didn't put myself out there. As I ventured out into the real world, I never felt like I had any idea of who I really was or what I wanted out of life, but that all changed when I got my first job as a social worker. I'd finally found something I excelled at—my something—my niche.

The work was challenging, and at times, I worried if I had what it took to deal with such hard demands, but I never gave up. I was determined to do my job and help the families I was working with to the best of my ability, and after just a few weeks, my supervisor started to take notice. Recognition wasn't something I was used to, but I liked it. I liked it a lot. It gave me the drive I needed to push through when times got tough—like the day I was first assigned to the Strayhorn case.

The cases I handled were always different. Some families were poor. Some were wealthy. Some had homes that were in complete shambles, while others lived in almost mansions. There wasn't a set of criteria that marked the people in my case files, so I tried to always expect the unexpected. I kept that in mind as I pulled up to the Strayhorn home. It was a pitiful sight. The paint was cracked and peeling, and there were boards covering several of the windows. As I got out of my car and started up the walkway, I became concerned when I noticed the boards on the front porch were severely warped making me fear that I might fall through the wooden planks. Doing my best to watch my footing, I made my way up to the door and knocked.

Moments later it opened, and my heart melted when I saw her—Fiona, the youngest of the Strayhorn children. Dark corkscrew ringlets framed her angelic face, and along with the sweetest little smile, she had the biggest brown eyes I'd ever seen. It looked like she was about to speak when a pained grimace crossed her face. She brought her hand up to her mouth, covering it as she started to cough. It sounded terrible, almost strangling her as she tried to catch her breath, making me wonder if the poor thing had pneumonia. When she finally caught her breath, I knelt down to her eye level and said, "Hi there, sweetheart. My name is Landry Dawson. I've come to check in on you and your brothers and sisters."

A worried expression crossed her face as she turned and looked over her shoulder, nervously checking to see if anyone was behind her. I knew it wasn't the first time someone had come to pay them a visit. I'd read over their records, and over the past eight months, there had been several calls and four DHS home visits. After several moments, she turned her attention back to me. When she didn't speak, I gave her a little push. "Is your mom around?"

"No." She tugged at the hem of her dingy t-shirt. "She's at work."

Her sweet little voice made me want to scoop her up in my arms and hold her as if she were my own. "What about your dad? Is he here?"

She shook her head. "No. Just my brudder, *Jo-sif*."

"Oh, okay." When I read over their file, there was no mention of either parent having a job. In fact, it showed that neither of them had worked in months. They were not only on unemployment but were also receiving food stamps. This wasn't an uncommon practice in the city, and I held no judgements in regards to their working situation as long as they were using the funds to provide for their family. I wasn't so sure that was happening, especially after reading about Joseph. On numerous accounts, he'd been caught stealing food from a nearby grocery store. Most thirteen-year-old boys would be trying to lift cigarettes instead of food, but after seeing his home and the sickly state of his youngest sister, I'd surmise that he'd grabbed what he could because he and his siblings were hungry. "Do you think you could go get Joseph? I'd really like to talk to him."

"Mm-hmm."

Leaving the door wide open, she turned and ran towards the center of the house. I stood up, then leaned forward, trying to get a better view of the inside. While the furniture was sparse, it seemed fairly clean—at least from what I could see of it. I was tempted to step inside but stayed put when I heard Fiona shout, "Jo-sif! A lady's here!"

"What?" he shouted in return.

"A lady's at da door!"

"Okay." I heard footsteps approaching, and just as he was about to reach the door, I heard him whisper to her, "Who is it?"

I tried to listen to her response, but it was muffled under another round of coughing. It was then that I realized Fiona wasn't the only one who was sick in the house. My concern was rising by the second, and when Joseph finally appeared at the door, it only grew higher. While adorably cute like his sister, he was very underweight, and there were dark circles under his eyes. He tried to put on a brave front, but I could hear the fear in his voice as he asked, "Can I help you with something?"

Printed in Great Britain
by Amazon